W9-CVO-126

BEASTLY CONFRONTATION

The Helghast yelled in fury as it saw that he had found the weapon, and sprang at him.

Lone Wolf rolled over, barely in control of his body's movements, and saw the creature's great clawed hands gouging out grooves of turf where he had lain only a moment before.

He forced himself to his knees and stabbed out blindly with the spear. He rapped the Helghast sharply on its side, but that was all.

It turned, on all fours, and stared at him with its infernal red eyes. Its lips were pulled well back from its fangs, and it drooled eagerly.

"Kill!" it barked gruffly, ready to spring. The words were rough around the edges, as if the creature had difficulty in mouthing them. "Kill in the name of Vono—"

The point of the spear cut deep into its cheek. Lone Wolf twisted the shaft, hoping to inflict a more serious wound, but the Helghast snapped its head away . . .

*The Legends of Lone Wolf series
from Berkley*

JOE DEVER'S
LEGENDS OF LONE WOLF

THE SWORD OF THE SUN

Book 4

JOE DEVER AND JOHN GRANT

Illustrated by Brian Williams

The Tides of Treachery and *The Sword of the Sun* were previously
published in one book entitled *The Sword of the Sun*

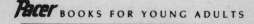 BOOKS FOR YOUNG ADULTS

BERKLEY BOOKS, NEW YORK

The Tides of Treachery and *The Sword of the Sun*
were previously published in one book entitled
The Sword of the Sun.

This Berkley / Pacer book contains the complete text
of the original edition. It has been
completely reset in a typeface designed for easy
reading and was printed from new film.

THE SWORD OF THE SUN

A Berkley / Pacer Book / published by arrangement with
Century Hutchinson, Ltd.

PRINTING HISTORY
Beaver Books edition published 1989
Berkley / Pacer edition / April 1991

ISBN: 0-425-12650-1

Pacer is a trademark belonging to The Putnam Publishing Group.

A BERKLEY / PACER BOOK ® TM 757,375
Berkley Books are published by the Berkley Publishing Group,
200 Madison Avenue, New York, New York 10016.
The name "Berkley" and the "B" logo are trademarks belonging to
Berkley Publishing Corporation.

PRINTED IN THE UNITED STATES OF AMERICA

10 9 8 7 6 5 4 3 2 1

For Hillary
and
Melinda

About the authors

JOE DEVER was born in 1956 at Woodford Bridge in Essex. After he left college, he became a professional musician, working in studios in Europe and America. While working in Los Angeles in 1977 he discovered a game called Dungeons and Dragons and was soon an enthusiastic player. Five years later he won the Advanced Dungeons and Dragons Championships in the USA, where he was the only British competitor. The award-winning series of *Lone Wolf* gamebooks were the culmination of many years' work developing the world of Magnamund. They are printed in several languages and sold throughout the world.

Joe also writes for modelling journals and contributes to Britain's leading role-playing games magazines. He adapts the Lone Wolf adventures for computer play, is editor of the *World of Lone Wolf* series, and is noted for his model painting and photography. He has recently begun to develop a new series of role-playing books, *Freeway Warrior*, which has met with considerable acclaim.

JOHN GRANT was born in 1949 in Aberdeen. He now lives in Exeter. Having studied math, physics and astronomy at London University, it was only natural that he should opt for a career in the arts, dividing his time between acting as an editor or editorial director for various publishing companies and being one of the world's least successful rock singer-songwriters. In recent years he has concentrated his efforts on editing and writing. His dozen or so books include *The Directory of Possibilities* (with Colin Wilson), *Dreamers, The Depths of Cricket, Earthdoom* (with David Langford), *Great Mysteries* and the vast *Encyclopedia of Walt Disney's Animated Characters*. He has also written countless articles, reviews, poems, short stories, parodies and humorous features, as well as appearing frequently on radio. His main interests are cricket and fantasy/science fiction: during the summer, when not writing, he bowls dangerously for a local cricket club. He is married to the artist Catherine Stewart, and they have a daughter.

CONTENTS

IN EARLIER DAYS. . .

Long, long before time itself began there were only the Gods and the void.

Throughout a timeless eternity there was war among the Gods, as Good and Evil sought to destroy each other. Neither could ever hope to succeed, and yet the struggle raged on . . .

The Goddess Ishir, High Priestess of the Moon, saw the futility of the conflict, and she made a truce with Naar, the King of the Darkness. Thus was brought about the Peace of Ishir. To acknowledge the truce, she shaped from the truth of her pledge a great vessel into which Naar infused the essence of his terrible power. This creation became Aon, the "Great Balance," a universe in which Good and Evil balanced each other.

The Gods were jealous of the worlds of Aon, and the Peace of Ishir was soon sundered. Here a world would be conquered by Evil, there another would be captured by Good. At last only one, Magnamund, remained unclaimed. Here Good and Evil met in a final confrontation.

First to enter Magnamund were the forces of Ishir's ally, Kai, Lord of the Sun. He sent beings which took the form of

1

giant sea dragons. The wisest of these was called Nyxator. Yet Naar, too, sent beings shaped as dragons to the oceans of Magnamund. Kai warned Nyxator of this and gave him great powers, which Nyxator was later to invest in artefacts known as the Lorestones. First the true dragons and then the false ones came on to the land, and for centuries there was war—a war won by the forces of Evil. Nyxator himself escaped and fled to Magnamund's molten core.

Naar could not rest until Nyxator was destroyed. After thousands of years he sent his most powerful servant, Agarash the Damned, to conquer Magnamund. Agarash created the Doomstones, a grotesque parody of the Lorestones. At last Agarash did battle with Nyxator at the core of the world, slew the aged dragon, and captured the Lorestones. Evil seemed triumphant, and Magnamund would have been lost had not Ishir and Kai introduced magic to the world.

Their creatures of magic, the Elder Magi, recaptured the Lorestones and, after a long and bloody war, crushed Agarash and his empire. Now began a time of peace, the Age of the Old Kingdoms, and many civilizations sprang up.

Nearly three thousand years later, by chance, a portal opened up between Magnamund and the astral world of Dazhiarn. Through this "Shadow Gate" came a race of lesser gods, the Shianti. After many centuries they encapsulated their knowledge and wisdom in a gem, the Moonstone, which had been shaped in Dazhiarn.

There was a Golden Age, during which many human civilizations appeared on the face of Magnamund. Yet all was not well: the presence of the Shianti adversely affected the balance between Good and Evil. Ishir came to the Shianti and told them of this. Reluctantly they surrendered the Moonstone back to Dazhiarn and exiled themselves to the remote Isle of Lorn.

A new race had sprung up, the Drakkarim, who took humanoid form yet were not of human stock. They terrorized the land, slaughtering all who stood in their way. Worse was to follow. Naar created new champions of Evil, the Darklords, and sent them into Magnamund. Swiftly the

Darklords, assisted by the Drakkarim, conquered vast tracts of Northern Magnamund.

In desperation Ishir and Kai sent forth a race of humans called the Sommlending, who had had their origins in islands to the north of mainland Magnamund. The Sommlending drove back the mightiest of the Darklords, Vashna, and came to occupy a small country, Sommerlund, adjacent to the seat of Vashna's greatest power, the arid, noxious territory known as the Darklands. Only a range of mountains, the Durncrags, separated Sommerlund from the evil emananting from the Darklands. The weapons of the Sommlending were—aside from those they forged themselves—their wisdom and their courage, as well as one given to them by the Gods of Good: the Sommerswerd, or "Sword of the Sun."

Aided by the Drakkarim, by lesser Darklords called the Xaghash, and by evil wizards known as the Nadziranim, Vashna constructed in the Darklands eight vast fortress-cities, the greatest of which was Helgedad. In Helgedad's dungeons he spawned vile creatures—Vordaks, Doomwolves, Kraan, Zlanbeast and Giaks. He created also the Helghast, who could adopt human form and mix among the Sommlending. However, they could be identified by the magicians of the Brotherhood of the Crystal Star, whose Guild resided in a city called Toran. The Sommerswerd was used to drive back the Helghast. At the Battle of Maakengorge, the Sommlending King Ulnar I slew Vashna, and in so doing lost his own life.

A Sommlending warrior who had distinguished himself at the Battle of Maakengorge was the Baron of Toran. He sought out the Lorestones, and in successfully doing so he unlocked the wisdom and strength that had been lying dormant within him. He became the first Kai Lord, taking the name of Sun Eagle, and founded a monastery where children of promise could be brought up so that their latent Kai powers could be developed fully. He recorded his experiences and new-found wisdom in the Book of the Magnakai.

The Darklords struggled among themselves for supremacy.

Just as Sun Eagle had discovered the Lorestones, they quested in search of the Doomstones, which had been lost in the mists of time. Success was achieved by the Darklord Zagarna, who, like Vashna, vowed to destroy Sommerlund. He launched an attack on the Kai Monastery, but the courage and prowess of the Kai were sufficient to repel his forces. Undeterred, he infiltrated and corrupted the royal courts of other human nations.

Still his greatest desire was the conquest of Sommerlund. In the year 5050 after the creation of the Moonstone a magician called Vonotar, eager to discover the secrets of the right-handed magic employed by the Nadziranim, fled from the Brotherhood of the Crystal Star to ally himself with Zagarna. The Darklord gave him these secrets in return for the information that each year, on the Feast of Fehmarn, the first day of Spring, all the Kai Lords congregated at their Monastery. Vonotar and Zagarna led a huge force of Giaks and other spawn, mounted on the bat-like Zlanbeast and Kraan, to destroy the Monastery and annihilate the Kai.

They nearly succeeded. Only one Kai, a young initiate called Silent Wolf, had been outside the Monastery when the dawn attack began. He had been urged to go and gather firewood as a result of the mental influence of an enigmatic elemental, Alyss. As he ran back through the trees to try to help his fellows, he hit his head on a low branch and was knocked unconscious. On coming to, he found that the massacre was over.

His life, too, would have been forfeit had not Alyss engaged Vonotar in a spiritual battle for long enough to allow Silent Wolf to escape the immediate vicinity of the carnage. The youth fled through the forest, his mission to reach the capital city, Holmgard, in order to inform King Ulnar V of the tragedy. Coming to a glade, he encountered a magician of roughly his own age doing battle with a platoon of Giaks. This was Banedon, a journeyman sent by the Guildmaster of the Brotherhood of the Crystal Star to warn the Kai of Vonotar's treachery. Silent Wolf drove off the Giaks, and the two of them declared their allegiance.

4

Banedon asked Silent Wolf his name, and the initiate told him that now, as he was the last of the Kai, he was taking to himself a new name: Lone Wolf.

The two of them separated, Lone Wolf heading for Holmgard and Banedon returning to Toran. By the time Banedon reached his destination, however, Toran was in ruins. Zagarna's vast army of Kraan had engineered a firestorm, which reduced the suburbs to a wasteland and the centre of Toran to a smouldering shambles. The Brotherhood of the Crystal Star, however, had survived, thanks to the intervention of Alyss, who had scotched a plot by Vonotar to destroy the Guild from within.

Lone Wolf took part in the Battle of Alema Bridge, almost saving the life of Prince Pelathar, the only son of King Ulnar. Pelathar with his dying breath urged Lone Wolf on to Holmgard, instructing him to tell the king that all that could now save Sommerlund was "that which is in Durenor"—the Sommerswerd. Lone Wolf accepted the mission and, after much peril, reached the capital, which was being besieged by Zagarna's armies.

A young woman called Qinefer, whose family had been slaughtered by Giaks, reached Holmgard shortly before Lone Wolf, and was ushered into the courtroom of King Ulnar's citadel. Initially Ulnar determined that she would be the one sent to fetch the Sommerswerd, but Lone Wolf and Qinefer agreed between them that he was the more experienced warrior and hence the better equipped to carry out the task; Qinefer acknowledged that she could best serve Sommerlund by helping defend Holmgard against the invaders.

The relationship between Vonotar and Zagarna was rapidly deteriorating, both of them intent on attaining sole control over all Magnamund. Yet they continued to work together in an uneasy partnership, both of them aware that, for the present, neither could do without the other. Besides, they had voluntarily linked their minds through the dark nothingness that was the soul-stuff of Naar, and they had no certain knowledge of what might happen were one of them to be destroyed.

5

Alyss had predicted that all three of "her" young people—Lone Wolf, Banedon and Qinefer—would contribute to the saving of Sommerlund, but Alyss had been known to lie whenever it suited her. As far as Lone Wolf was concerned, he was acting on his own—Banedon he dismissed as an incompetent, Qinefer as nothing more than a promising warrior for the future.

Lone Wolf set sail for Durenor aboard the Green Sceptre, *a swift caravel, but sabotage storms, and shipwreck soon put paid to his hopes of a speedy voyage. Then a deadly encounter with cutthroats in the sleazy city-port of Ragadorn very nearly brought his life to a premature close. Had it not been for Alyss's supernatural intervention, the young Kai Lord would have ended his days facedown in the murky waters of Ragadorn quay.*

Determined still to fulfill his quest, Lone Wolf now travels a new road to Durenor aboard a coach bound for Port Bax.

1

THE ROAD TO DURENOR

1

For three hours the coach trundled along the muddy coast road without slowing until, at last, the outline of a toll bridge appeared in the middle distance. Rain made the window into a grey slate through which Lone Wolf could only just see the toll-collector, who was a Szall—a breed of Giak no more harmful than a domestic cat. Nevertheless, Lone Wolf felt his hand wandering towards his dagger: it had become a natural instinct for him to slay Giaks, wherever he found them. It was with difficulty that he restrained himself, especially when he saw his fellow-passengers passing money across to pay the creature. As a matter of principle he refused to produce any money; the Szall waited for a few long loneful moments outside the window of the coach before finally shrugging and giving up.

The interruption had made Lone Wolf begin to recognize that there were other people aboard the coach, and, once he'd studied them, he wasn't too pleased that this was so. Sitting opposite him, he discovered, were two brothers, Ganon and Dorier, who were knights of the Order of the White Mountain: they were warrior lords from Durenor who had pledged allegiance to protect the country from raids by the bandits of the Wildlands. Lone Wolf forced himself to converse brightly with them. Sitting beside them was a merchant called Halvorc; his nose was swollen and his face badly bruised thanks, it turned out during the conversation the passengers exchanged among themselves, to a little disagreement with Lachlan. By Lone Wolf's side there was a mercenary soldier called Viveka; he was conscious of her femininity, which was oddly enhanced by a deep scar that ran down the side of her face from the lobe of her left ear to the point of her chin. And over on the far side of the coach there was a priest called Parsion: Lone Wolf recognized him immediately as another Sommlending.

Parsion and Ganon were chatting about the invasion of Sommerlund, and Lone Wolf very quickly realized that their information was both scanty and badly distorted. Clearly the word-of-mouth stories of merchants and travellers had become much garbled in the telling. Lone Wolf heard how the war had started when Ulnar had sent a great army to assault Zagarna's stronghold at Kaag, and how the Darklord had therefore been quite justified in retaliating with his murderous hordes. There were tales, too, of sadistic butchery of Drakkarim by the Sommlending people: roasting alive and subsequent feasting on the flesh were the less lurid elements of these stories. In fact, so unfavourable to the Sommlending was much of this stuff that Lone Wolf began to reappraise his earlier assumption: perhaps it was not just that some fairly gaudy initial stories had been embellished in the bars of Ragadorn; more likely, it seemed, was that Zagarna or someone close to him had sent emissaries into the Wildlands, in the form of Helghast or renegade humans, to spread disinformation about what was going on. If this idea was correct, Lone Wolf reflected, then it was very alarming, because it indicated that Zagarna's sights were indeed set on the domination of all Magnamund.

"Do you believe much of all that?" he said conversationally to Viveka, nodding towards Parsion and Ganon.

"That dross? You have to be joking." Her voice was mellow and sweet, like her appearance a rugged contrast with her cruel trade. "You don't have to like the Sommlending—and I've little love for them, myself—to know that they're just the first to feel the brunt of Zagarna's hatred for all of humankind. Why do you think I'm going back to Port Bax? Ragadorn's going to be next. Mark my words."

"I'm a Sommlending myself," Lone Wolf muttered.

"That's pretty obvious," the mercenary replied with a smile; the movement of her face twisted the scar into an impossible shape. "I can dislike the Sommlending as a whole and still like individual members of your race. You're OK, my friend; I could tell that as soon as you climbed aboard this coach."

"You seem to be a mite selective in your appraisal of us Sommlending. I'm just a peasant who finds himself here, far from home when I hear these tales of war—"

"Rot!"

"Sorry?"

"'Rot,' I said. You're no more a peasant than I am. Whatever it is that's going on in Sommerlund—and I wonder if it's really a war or just another of those infernal skirmishes you people conduct with the Darklands—I can sense that you've got something to do with it. You haven't just climbed on this coach because you chose to visit Durenor on some kind of whim—you've got some reason, and I reckon it's something to do with Ulnar's ambitions to bring down Zagarna."

Lone Wolf was appalled by the penetration of her insight. Was it so obvious to everybody what he was?

She laughed.

"You're very young. Everything you think is written on your face. Now you're wondering if I'm a friend or an enemy. Well, I'm a friend of yours so long as it suits me. And that'll have to be enough for your curiosity right now!"

She turned away from him, wriggled down into her seat, and within moments was asleep. He looked out of the window and saw the drab scenery trickling by. The murmur of his companions' conversation drifted on around him. Viveka began to snore, very gently, in a way that was definitely lady-like. He found himself abominably attracted to this woman yet he recognized that she was a mercenary who would sell his soul quite happily, if it pleased her so to do. She was yet another conundrum—something he could do without. But it was disturbing that she seemed to know so much about him. Was he *that* transparent?

He found himself drowsing, half-awake and half-asleep, so that sometimes the dull, uninspired scenery he was watching became painted with brilliant colours and contorted itself into bestial forms; whenever that happened he'd realize that he was drifting into sleep and, by sheer effort of will-power, drag himself back to wakefulness. He wasn't the only passenger who was finding the steady thump of the horses' hooves and the trundle of the coach over the rough road soporific, he knew: the two brothers had drifted off, as had the priest. Only the merchant, Halvorc, seemed to be wide awake; his battered face was absorbed in a book, and he moved easily with the rocking of the coach. When Lone Wolf looked across at him the man was instantly aware of his gaze, and looked back, his pale-blue eyes intent. Lone Wolf turned away, embarrassed.

At dusk they stopped at an inn. Clearly it was somewhere near to the coast because, although they couldn't see the sea, they could hear the crashing of waves in the middle distance. Lone Wolf shuddered, remembering how the waves had smashed against him as he lay, clinging tenuously to life, on the hatch cover.

Stiffly the passengers hauled themselves out of the

coach, and the driver checked their tickets perfunctorily. The cost of a bed for the night, he muttered to each of them, speaking the words by rote because he'd spoken them a thousand times before, was a gold crown, and if they didn't have the money they were perfectly welcome to sleep in the coach. Lone Wolf reluctantly produced the money; despite the innkeeper's generosity, his funds were once again running low. Tonight he could sleep in a warm bed, but for the rest of the journey he might be better off opting for the coach.

The inn was badly furnished but it was at least cozily warm, and Lone Wolf had few complaints about the vast meal which the equally vast landlady placed in front of them. He went to bed early and slept soundly, waking at dawn feeling deeply refreshed. He dressed and ate a good breakfast, joking easily with his fellow-passengers, before they climbed aboard the coach once more.

The same pattern was repeated for the next couple of days and nights, although, as he had determined, Lone Wolf took to sleeping in the coach in order to conserve his funds. On the second night Ganon and Dorier did likewise, and their snoring kept Lone Wolf awake much of the time, so that in the morning his throat felt raw and his head throbbed. He vowed that, economy or not, he would allow himself the luxury of a bed in whatever inn they stopped at that evening.

The morning meandered on. Parsion and the two brothers kept up an incessant flow of chatter, Halvorc read one of the seemingly endless supply of books he had brought with him, and Lone Wolf and Viveka divided their time between aimless exchanges of trivial conversation and dozing.

Lone Wolf was dreaming that he was fleeing for his life through the countless dungeons of some nameless castle when he was shocked into wakefulness.

The world was being thrown from side to side. He was buffeted from beneath by his seat. Viveka was thrown against him, and he saw her face quite differently; those

11

elegant features were twisted into an animal snarl. Halvorc, very unexpectedly, was screaming in terror.

Loud cracking sounds. More battering. A last crunch. Then silence except for the cursing of the driver and the frightened whimpering of the horses. The coach was canted over to one side, and swayed uneasily as Lone Wolf moved to the window.

"What's going on?" he shouted at the driver.

He was rewarded with a torrent of abuse, in which he was able to pick out two words: "wheel" and "broken." To his surprise, Viveka beside him responded with a similar stream of profanity, the obscenities jarring with her well modulated accent.

They scrambled out of the coach with some difficulty, finding themselves on a rocky track. They were in the middle of a desolate plain, the dreary vista broken only by occasional blackened trees, which bent creakingly when caught by the stiff breeze. Brownish-green mosses covered the land as far as they could see.

At some time in the past couple of weeks it must have rained torrentially. Since then the weak spring sunshine had baked the mud of the road, so that its ruts and bumps had dried stone-hard. The rear left wheel of the coach had snarled in one of the rigid ruts and its rim and three of its spokes had snapped off just below the hub. The coach stood crazily on its remaining three wheels, looking as if a giant had dropped it from the sky.

The driver had succeeded in calming his horses, and came round to join his passengers in assessing the damage. He was still cursing fluently, but his tones were gentler now and he flashed a grin at them.

"Often happens on this trip," he said. "Trouble is, I can never tell exactly where or when."

"How are we going to get to Port Bax?" asked the merchant. He had controlled the worst of his fears, but his voice was still tremulous.

"Not to worry too much, sir," said the driver reassuringly. "We always carry spare wheels on this route. Got a couple of them strapped on below, here." He pointed with his booted toe to the underside of the coach. "If some of you could find a branch to help me lever this blasted old crate level, I'll have a new wheel on her in no time."

Lone Wolf and Viveka volunteered, and trudged off across the plain towards the nearest of the dead-looking trees. The mercenary's face had lost that mindless fury which Lone Wolf had seen flash briefly during the accident, and she moved with a girlish easiness, her sword swinging at her side.

"Quite an adventure," she said easily. "Breaks up the tedium of the day, doesn't it?"

"Suppose it does," he said dourly, unable to imitate her lightness of spirit.

"I wonder if it was sabotage?" she said, without changing her tone but looking at him sharply.

"Don't see how it could be." He realized that he was speaking rudely, and apologized with a shrug. The problem was that exactly the same question had been going through his own mind.

"Just how important *is* this mission of yours?" she asked.

"Not very," he lied.

"You sure?"

"Course I am."

"Hmm. It just struck me that perhaps someone might be trying to delay you."

They had reached the tree, and she was looking at it critically.

"Don't see how they could have arranged . . . this." He gestured towards the scene of the crippled coach on the baked road.

"The driver might have. Skilled fellow like him. Waited for the right rut to come along and then driven deliberately straight into it. *Splick!*" She jabbed her upright hand straight in front of her, as if it was being guided by a twisty rail. "Easy as anything, for a good horseman."

"True. But I can't really see it. Can you?"

"To tell you the truth: no. But there's something about this journey that's disquieting me, and I don't know what it is—except that every time I start to think about it *you* seem to be at the centre of my thoughts."

"We'd better cut a branch. Here, let me have your sword."

"You're not hacking wood with this blade, my friend," she said. "My life depends on keeping it sharp, and I'm uncommonly keen on preserving my life. But I'll let you change the subject, if that's what you want. Only—only, any time you feel like talking about it, let me know, eh?"

He looked into her eyes and saw no trace of guile. She seemed to be being utterly frank. And yet he knew that she could hardly be trusted . . . but at the same time he believed that she could. *Your wits are in a bit of a mess about this*, he thought to himself angrily, *and it's only because she's so good-looking. Durnflies look good, too, but you know they're poisonous and you keep well clear of them. Best to treat this woman the same way.*

"I don't blame you," she said.

"What? I mean, what for?"

"For not wanting to trust me. I wouldn't trust me myself, if I didn't know me so well. But, for what it's worth, and believe me or not as you decide, you can trust me for as long as this journey lasts."

This was all too weighty for Lone Wolf.

"Let's get that branch," he said.

"Right you are." She swung into movement, looking for all the world as if they'd just been discussing nothing more profound than the weather. "Let me have your mace."

The mace wasn't the most subtle of implements, but it was effective enough for their purposes. Taking turns, they had soon pounded a long sturdy branch away from the tree's main trunk. They swung it up on their shoulders and, Viveka leading the way, stumbled back to the coach.

The driver had loosed one of the spare wheels, and was

balancing it upright on the road with one hand, his stubby fingers lying almost gracefully on its rim. He looked at Lone Wolf and Viveka approvingly as they approached with the branch.

"Right," he said, "if you good people would help me we shouldn't be delayed long."

Halvorc was deputed to hold the spare wheel—more, Lone Wolf suspected, to give him something to do to take his mind off his recent terrors than for any real reason of practicality—while Viveka and Lone Wolf were shown how to use the log to hoist the rear of the carriage level. The work wasn't particularly onerous, shared as it was between the two of them, although Lone Wolf looked on somewhat sceptically as the driver crouched directly underneath the rear axle, wrestling with the broken wheel: the whole set-up seemed dangerously precarious to him, but he assumed the man must know what he was doing.

Parsion and the two brothers had drifted off somewhere, leaving them to get on with it, and Lone Wolf wished that there was some way that Halvorc could do the same. He was beginning to find the presence of his fellow-passengers, with the exception of Viveka, a constantly niggling irritation. Even about Viveka he had somewhat ambiguous feelings: on the one hand he was drawn to her, and enjoyed being in her company; on the other, there was something about her which he knew that he didn't fully understand, and it made him decidedly uneasy. He couldn't decide whether she . . .

A sudden engulfing sound. Screams of panic torn from the horses' throats. A blow in the face, hurtling him flat on the ground. Tumbling noises and colours, all mixed up, so that he saw the noises and heard the colours. Splintering wood. Now a yell of anguish from someone. Himself?—no, someone else. Mouth aching, nose aching, all of head aching. Darkness—briefly only. Swimming along a seemingly endless tunnel, back into the light. Got to get there, got to get there . . . Forcing

15

himself up on his elbow, then the much longer and more dangerous climb to his feet.

"What? What? What?" he said stupidly, clutching his jaw.

"Shut up and help me here, you blithering idiot," snapped Viveka. She was kneeling down, her fine hair thrown back over her shoulder, her attention fixed on an oddly shaped bundle on the ground. The merchant was whining inanely, but she ignored him.

Confusedly Lone Wolf lurched to her side. "Help," he said. "Help you . . . how?"

"I don't think there's much help either of us can give," she said grimly. Now Lone Wolf could see that the bundle on the ground was the driver, his body looking as if someone had tried to beat it right into the rock-hard surface of the road. There was a lot of blood on his chest and face, and his clothes were half-shredded away.

"What happened?" said Lone Wolf, his mind beginning to work properly again.

"The horses bolted. This poor fellow was underneath the coach, and the thing collapsed on top of him. The broken spokes went right into him."

"My face—"

"The branch sprang up and the end of it caught you right on the chin. Do you know anything about healing?"

"Only a little," said Lone Wolf. His powers were limited and flighty, he knew, but he tried to summon them now. He put his hands on the driver's beaten forehead and attempted to channel some of his own body's strength through his fingers into the man. There was some feeling of draining energy, but only a little—not nearly enough, he knew. Still, he forced himself to continue, striving to make some sort of breakthrough, silently calling upon Ishir and Kai to come to his assistance. He made rash promises to them of future good deeds, but the Gods chose not to respond, and he knew that the man's life was ebbing away as clearly as if he could see it flowing out on the roadway.

"I'm sorry," he said exhaustedly, "not enough . . . can't—" He slumped.

The driver recovered consciousness briefly, and looked up at the faces of Lone Wolf and Viveka. His eyes showed no pain, only a desperate eagerness to communicate something to them. He moved his broken mouth with obvious difficulty as he tried to push words out between his lips.

"No—no accident," he said thickly. "I saw . . . "

But then his last resources of strength failed him and his body seemed to fold in on itself, quite calmly. The two of them continued to watch his face for a few seconds longer, and then Viveka got to her feet, brushing her knees distractedly.

"He saw something," she said bitterly.

"Or some*one*."

"True, could have been a person. And we're the only people around here. You and I were holding the log and Halvorc had the wheel, so it could hardly have been any of us . . . it must have been one of the other three."

Ganon, Dorier and Parsion were about twenty yards further down the road, where they had succeeded in subduing the horses. The merchant had scuttled to join them, and his hands were flying as he told them over and over again the dreadful calamity that had befallen them, and he'd been *so* close himself, hardly a whisker away from doom, less than a whisker in fact, and . . . Her eyes ranged over them thoughtfully.

Lone Wolf had difficulty thinking straight because of the pain in his face, but it seemed to him that there were some loopholes in Viveka's chain of reasoning. He remembered the ancient man he had seen flying high in the skies above the wrecking of the *Green Sceptre*, and he wondered if perhaps that sorcerer had played some part in this "accident" as well. He looked around but could see no signs of him—although that meant nothing, of course: anyone with sufficient magical ability to fly would have little trouble in rendering himself invisible.

At a more mundane level, there was somebody else who could have caused the disaster—Viveka herself. He looked at her trim, muscular form and remembered the speed and ease with which he'd seen her move, when it suited her. She could have pulled the log away abruptly from beneath the coach, simultaneously knocking him senseless with it and letting the vehicle drop. That could easily have been enough to startle the horses . . . except the whole scenario didn't quite add up. If he was the target of the sabotage—and he was convinced that he was, because something or someone had been dogging his path ever since he'd left Holmgard on this disaster-strewn quest—then Viveka could hardly have done anything less calculated to take his life. Or was that true? The blow to his face had been a very severe one; might it have been calculated to break his neck? He looked again at Viveka, and once more dismissed the thought: the woman was a mercenary, and there was a calm efficiency about everything she did. If she'd wanted to hit him hard enough to kill him she'd have done it. There wouldn't have been any mistake.

It crossed his mind, not for the first time, that it would be a good thing if it "suited" Viveka to be his friend for quite a long time—as long as possible, in fact.

"You know," she said, "I'm becoming very interested in the importance of you and your mission, young man. Very interested indeed."

She gazed at him levelly.

"What makes you say that?"

"Because somebody tried to kill you, just then. I'm convinced of it. And nobody would be trying to kill you if you weren't of some importance."

"They might have been trying to kill *you*," Lone Wolf protested. "You were as vulnerable as I was."

This was obviously a brand-new thought to her, and she mulled it over, not liking it much.

"No . . . " she said slowly. "No, I can't really see that. There's no cause that anyone should want me

dead. There've been a few, of course, but . . . well"—
she laughed suddenly—"obviously they're dead themselves, now."

He saw the ruthlessness in her. It frightened him.

"Your king might pay me well for your continued safe-
ty," she went on.

"Might he?"

"Possibly. I'll take a gamble on it. Between here and
Port Bax, young man, you'll have an extra pair of eyes
looking out for your well-being."

They went to join the others.

2

Up here in the topmost room of the Guildhall of the
Brotherhood of the Crystal Star, one could look out over
the whole of Toran and see how already the city was being
restored to its original form after its virtual destruction
by fire and Zagarna's flying hordes. Dutifully men and
women were measuring out the exact positions of all
the original streets, side streets, squares and back alleys.
Some citizens had proposed that here was a unique chance
to redesign the city, to restructure it completely, but this
had been overruled by the Brotherhood's Guildmaster,
who had pointed out that the original configuration had
been accurately calculated to form a part of Toran's magical defences. As he had forcibly argued to a meeting of
his fellow Guildmasters, had it not been for this pattern
of lines and angles, often apparently crazy, but all drawn
up according to the principles of left-handed magic as
devised by the brothers and sisters of his Guild, the city
might have been razed to the ground—there might have
been nothing left of it to reconstruct.

Banedon stood in the window, watching the scene of
activity, his youthful face etched with new lines born
from his sorrow and guilt. From time to time he glanced
across at a plain cot in the corner, where Alyss's physical

body lay motionless, neither breathing nor decaying, as if frozen into a single slice of time. For the past few days he had been keeping this vigil by her side, eating and sleeping in her presenceless presence, leaving his post only when his bladder or his bowels forced him to. He wanted more than anything he had wanted in his life before to see her eyelids flicker, or her thin chest to start moving in the natural rhythms of life. He refused to believe that she was dead, whatever some of the sceptics among the brothers might say: somewhere, but who could tell where, her spirit was still alive—and would one day return to the shell of the body which she had chosen to adopt.

They had carried her up here after the traumatic time of her restoration of Lone Wolf's life. They had wrapped her form solemnly in white sheets, moving as if controlled by something beyond themselves, hardly conscious of what they were doing. The long windows of this high room allowed the sun to play across her features whenever it climbed out from behind the clouds. The sun—its healing influence blanketed her right now, picking out the height of her cheekbones and the redness of her rusty cropped hair. Banedon felt that somehow, through those closed eyelids, he could see the greenness of her eyes, and that those eyes were moving; but every time he moved towards her, intending to push back the eyelids and see for himself that she lived, something held him back—a physical force which he couldn't understand.

She was somewhere, he recognized, between life and death. If he'd known where that "somewhere" was, he would have gone there and beseeched her spirit to return, but his magical abilities were strictly limited; even the Guildmaster, through whose veins swam a crackling current of pure left-handed energy, had been unable to locate the somewhere/nowhere in which Alyss's spirit was now closeted.

There were times when Banedon found himself agreeing with those of the Brotherhood who said that there was no point in all this, that Alyss was dead and there was nothing more that could be done about it. Then he would look at her waxen face and recall how animated it had been, and he would decline to believe the cynics.

Somewhere, out there somewhere, she surely still existed!

Ah, yes, but where?

And he said to himself, silently, *I have come to love you, Alyss. Please return to us if only for that.*

But, just as it had a million times before when he had thought those words, Alyss's body reacted not at all.

3

Parsion, the priest, initially dictated their actions.

"We must bury this man," he said. "A tragedy—but more of a tragedy if we don't consign his soul to Ishir."

Lone Wolf agreed silently. The driver had, as it were, died for him. The least the man could be accorded was a burial. He looked mutely at Viveka and she gave him a sorry half-smile in return. Without speaking to each other they picked up the branch which they'd used to lever up the coach and carried it to a piece of soft ground, perhaps twenty yards from the road. They used its splintered end to dig into the earth. Lone Wolf found himself pushing against it with bitterness. Everywhere he went, it seemed, there was a trail of meaningless death: he wished that the torment would stop, but he sensed that it would continue until Zagarna was dead—or, perhaps even more important, until the enigmatic old man he had seen in the skies had been killed.

The grave was a shallow one. Lone Wolf and Viveka reached a level beneath the surface of the soil where, no matter how hard they scraped, they seemed incapable of digging any deeper. They bundled the driver's body into it, nevertheless, and the priest said a few words which were swept away so swiftly by the wind that no one could tell what they were. All five of them helped scoop the earth back over the man's body, even the merchant participating. There was nothing more that they could do except stare for a moment of silence out across the bleakness of the plain, wishing that in the last couple of days they'd somehow been kinder, friendlier, towards the man whose corpse was even now cooling at their feet.

They were in little mood for conversation as they walked back to the damaged coach.

"I know the road from here to Port Bax," said Halvorc hesitantly. "I've been this way several times before. I'll drive the coach if you like—assuming we can replace the wheel."

No one else volunteered to drive. Lone Wolf shivered as the cold crept under his clothing.

"We can put the other wheel on," said Viveka after a while. "I was watching what the driver was doing. It shouldn't be too hard."

"I'll help," said Lone Wolf immediately, and she nodded, as if she'd already taken his help for granted.

"So will my brother and I," said Ganon. Dorier made a forced smile of assent, but then his face slowly relaxed again as he realized that this wasn't a time for smiling.

"We'll all have to help," said Viveka.

She directed Halvorc to control the horses. Lone Wolf recognized the shrewdness of the move: apart from the two of them, Halvorc was the only other person who'd been in no position to make the horses bolt. Dorier and Ganon used the branch to lever the coach up and Parsion grappled with the extra wheel while she and Lone Wolf, moving as nimbly as the cold permitted, wrenched the wreckage of the old wheel away from its axle and replaced it. The whole process took them not more than half an hour.

Halvorc clambered awkwardly up at the front and took the reins; Ganon climbed up beside him to act as deputy driver. The other four got inside the coach, sitting as far apart from each other as they could, looking everywhere but into each other's eyes.

Parsion was shaking all over.

"When we get to Port Bax, you know," he said nervously, "they're going to ask us about what happened to the driver. They'll maybe say that it was all our fault. Perhaps they'll think that we murdered him." He fiddled the fingers of his two hands together, and seemed to be praying.

"Nonsense!" cried Dorier, pounding his fist against the wooden door next to him. "I was there—me and my brother. We're Knights of the White Mountain, you know. We can testify that it was an accident, nothing more."

"I could say as much," muttered the priest, "but would they *believe* me?"

Dorier punched the roof and shouted his brother's name.

Ganon responded with an irritated yell. He was trying to sort out which rein was which, because Halvorc seemed to have little idea.

"The priest thinks the authorities in Port Bax might not believe our story," cried Dorier.

"Then he's a dimwit," Ganon replied caustically. "Only don't tell him that."

The priest's sallow face uncharacteristically reddened.

"What does he mean?" he hissed.

"You don't know much about Durenor, do you?" said Viveka.

"No," said the priest.

"If you did, you'd know about the oaths of the knights."

"What oaths?"

"Oh, there are many of them." An airy wave of her hand, indicating huge but unspecified numbers. "One of the most important is the Oath of Truthfulness. The various orders of knights in Durenor, including the—what did you say your order was again?"

"The Knights of the White Mountain," said Dorier stiffly.

"Yes, them too. When they're sworn into the order they have to vow that for the rest of their lives they'll speak the truth at all times, even if it brings down the wrath of the Gods on their heads."

Lone Wolf interrupted. "It's easy enough to take an oath," he said, "and even easier to break it."

"Not for a knight of Durenor, it isn't," said Viveka. "If any of them's caught in a lie—even a tiny one, like 'My, you're looking well today'—he's likely to face public execution. Personally I think it's idiocy, but that's the way they do things in Durenor. I've always found lying extremely useful, myself."

Lone Wolf was reminded of someone, but he couldn't think who it was.

"So you see," said Dorier reassuringly to the priest, "Ganon and I will tell exactly what we saw—that it was all just a dreadful mischance."

And truth is a relative thing, thought Lone Wolf. *Assuming that your brother and yourself are indeed the honest knights you seem to be—and I'm by no means convinced of that— then you'll tell the truth about what you saw. But that needn't be the whole truth—not the reality of the situation. It'll be just what you think* happened, *and you won't even know that you're telling a lie. But I'll know, and Viveka will, because someone tried to kill me here, and whoever it was will try again, and next time maybe they'll succeed, and you'll tell the "truth" about another mysterious accident which you witnessed . . .*

The coach was beginning to move. At first the horses were restive, recognizing Halvorc for the inexperienced driver he was, but soon they settled back into their normal steady pace, and the vehicle bowled along smoothly enough. Its movement seemed to soothe the worries of the priest, because he nestled himself back into the stale-smelling upholstery of the seat and closed his eyes. Dorier looked out of the window, apparently counting the trees as they went by, drumming his fingers on the panelling as if he were impatient, now, to reach Port Bax as soon as possible. Lone Wolf controlled his own impatience, and just allowed his thoughts to run free for a while;

then he turned and looked at Viveka and they smiled at each other. Impulsively he took her hand in his and, after a moment's hesitation, she relaxed her fingers, so that they linked lightly through his. It was a curiously maternal gesture from a woman whose whole persona radiated hardness and efficiency, but it comforted Lone Wolf and he allowed himself to relax. He had an ally, a protector . . . at least for a while.

4

Evening was drawing pastel greys across the sky when they came to a down-at-heel village which straggled lethargically along the sides of the road. Halvorc reined in the horses as they arrived at a barren expanse of openness which obviously served as the main square. To their left they could see through the gaps between the houses some rugged cliffs and the angry lashings of the waves combing in from the Gulf of Durenor. Ahead of them a bridge crossed an oily expanse of water.

A couple of Szalls approached the coach cautiously, and once again Lone Wolf felt the urgent need to slay these Giaks. He took his hand away from Viveka's and clenched it tightly in front of him. He had to remember that the Szalls were only pale shadows of the vicious beasts which formed the bulk of Zagarna's armies. These creatures were too timid to risk the vengeance they might incur if they were to attack a human being.

Ganon, perched high in front of the coach, chattered with the Szalls rapidly. Lone Wolf could make out only a few of the words. Then the knight hopped down and rapped on the window.

"We've got a choice," he said cheerfully. "Either we can stay the night here in this dump—Gorn Cove, they call it—or we can keep going and camp out somewhere along the road. The next place of any size is Port Bax itself, about fifty miles away, so there's no chance of making it tonight."

"Doesn't seem like much of a choice to me," his brother said. He looked around the others, and they nodded in agreement. "Guess we'll have to slop ourselves into all the nameless debaucheries of Gorn Cove's nightlife—the lady permitting," he added, with a mock bob of his head towards Viveka.

"I hardly dare trust my virtue to this hotbed of rampant sin," she said drily, letting her eyes rove across the parched drabness of the place. "I wouldn't put it past them to play nude samor here."

"Ah, samor," said Parsion, sucking in his thin lips. "A sinful game, that is."

"We're agreed, then?" asked Ganon, making a face. "I should warn you that the only inn here, according to the locals, is such a wild attraction that they call it the Forlorn Hope."

"My mother told me about places like that," said Viveka.

Whoever had named the Forlorn Hope had been desperately optimistic. The slimy corridor which served as its entrance hall echoed with the undisturbed filth of the years. The six of them clattered in, helping each other with their packages and trunks, and looked around them in dismay.

"I think I'd prefer the nude samor," muttered Viveka after a pause.

They were met by a thin old man, who stared at them with welcoming disapproval through his single eye. This was clearly their landlord; behind them, from the foul-smelling kitchens, they could hear shouted imprecations and obscenities and the clattering of pots and pans.

"You be the coach-load from Ragadorn?" asked the landlord, with a woeful attempt at geniality. "*Shut your trap, woman!*" he added in the direction of the kitchens. "And I assume you'll be wanting six single rooms?"

26

He looked pointedly at Viveka as he said this, and her eyes flared.

"Four single rooms," she said with carefully controlled quietness. "My brother and I will share."

Parsion and Halvorc looked shocked, Ganon and Dorier leered, and Lone Wolf felt his jaw drop.

"As the *lady* pleases." The landlord winked conspiratorially at Lone Wolf. *"Belt up, you stupid bitch, or I'll rearrange your face! Just a bit of friendly marital banter,"* he explained. "I'd help you with your bags, but there's an 'r' in the month and so my back's playing me up something rotten. *And your mother's face as well if she comes round here!"*

"Look, what are you playing at?" whispered Lone Wolf to Viveka, as they struggled up the dilapidated stairs in the wake of the landlord's skinny rump. "I'm not your brother, for the sake of Ishir! The rest of the people will be thinking that—"

"I don't much care what they think," said Viveka shortly. "From here until we reach Port Bax you're my brother. It's the only way that I can keep my eye on you, like I said I would." She paused halfway up the stairs. "I should request you not to take advantage of the situation." Narrow, threatening eyes.

"Of course not. But you might have warned me." Lone Wolf strangled a few mildly interesting speculations at birth.

"I'm sorry, brother. I'll remember in future, brother. Too silly of me, brother. Now shut up and start being my brother, blast you!"

They had a balcony room, through the window of which they could see the deserted remnants of an open-cast mine, "a fascinating example of industrial archaeology," as Viveka described it. The room was L-shaped, and Lone Wolf was relieved to see that its two single beds were separated from each other by the angle of the "L." The beds themselves were in a quite dangerously rickety condition, and Viveka tested both of them by bouncing on them before choosing for herself the safer. "I think we should be comfortable enough here," she lied bitterly.

There was a rat-a-tat-tat on the door, and Dorier shouted through it.

"If the siblings are agreeable, perhaps we could meet in the bar in an hour's time to talk about what we should do tomorrow."

"This sibling agrees," said Viveka cheerfully, looking dubiously into a vast porcelain jug which had been placed by the bedside. "My brother says it's all right, too."

"Viveka," Lone Wolf said once Dorier's footsteps had retreated, "you'll excuse me for saying this, and of course I know you're acting only for the best, but I object to the fact that you seem to be taking over my life."

"Thought you might. This water's scummy."

"I don't think you're supposed to drink it—I think it's for washing yourself in. Actually, it was quite a good idea of yours that we should share a room, but it was a bit much just springing it on me. You could at least have consulted me."

"I wasn't going to drink it, you clot. I don't know what your standards of hygiene are, and I'm not much sure that I want to find out, but I wouldn't wash a rat in this unless it had severely offended me. It was only at the last minute that I suddenly realized it would make a lot of sense if I were able to keep my eyes on you at night as well as during the day. I wonder if that landlord would charge me extra if I asked him for some fresh water?"

"Probably not. No, on second thought, from what I've seen of him so far, he probably would. But that's not the important thing. The fact is that I don't think I need your protection. I've survived this long without anyone to help me"—he struggled out of his shirt and lay back on his bed, luxuriating in the feel of the cool blankets against his shoulder blades—"and I think that, thank you very much, I can keep on doing so."

"Someone among us is trying to kill you," said Viveka, opening the window and tipping the stagnant water out on the straggly, weed-choked garden below. "Until we find out who that person is, you need someone to guard you. And I wouldn't be so cocky about how tough you are, brother, because I reckon I could break you in half if I really wanted to." She turned away from him to hang up her gear—mainly heavy items of weaponry—in a rudimentary wardrobe.

Viveka vanished from the room for a minute, bearing the empty jug, then reappeared, holding it more carefully. "No problem at all getting fresh water," she announced. "Funny the way that men are always so quick to see sense when you've got your hands round their throat. Now, where were we? Ah, yes. You're going to be my little brother for as long as it takes us to get to Port Bax. After that you can choose your own way of dying. Now, if you'll excuse me, I'd like to wash some of the dust of the day off me."

She twisted her hand in the air and Lone Wolf dutifully turned away. He let his eyes close. Holmgard seemed a very long way away, and he was hungry for the security of someone he could trust completely. Viveka was a friend, he felt pretty certain of it, but he wasn't certain that he could trust her entirely—if someone offered her a bag of gold crowns right now, she might easily turn on him, slaughter him and pocket the fee. Besides, she seemed to be playing games with him, and he resented that.

After what seemed a very long time she told him that it was all right to look round again. By then his thoughts were swirling in a peculiarly warm and pleasing fashion, and he mumbled that he'd rather lie here a while longer. He was only dimly aware of the sounds of her leaving the room—of her telling him firmly that he was expected down in the taproom in fifteen minutes to join the rest of them—as he found that, with only a gentle manipulation of his imagination, he could find himself swimming deeply in a clear sea, surrounded by clusters of brilliantly coloured fishes, feeling the warm water's cleanness washing all the way through him . . .

He was pulled out of his dreams by a knocking on the door. It took him a few minutes to remember where he was, but then he tumbled himself off his bed and groped his way unsteadily through the gloom to find the door.

He opened it, and his eyes shrank from the brightness of the corridor beyond.

Framed in the door was the crooked figure of the inn-keeper. The slight, twisted man was clutching a wooden tray, on which there was a bowl of steaming stew.

"Your friend sent this up to you, sir," he said, "seeing as you're late for supper down below. *I wouldn't care if your mother was the king of all the Giaks herself, I'd still use her guts for a catapult!* Pardon me, but it's just me and the wife's way of expressing our affection. We have our little customs."

Lone Wolf nodded dumbly, and took the tray of food. He hadn't noticed being hungry before, but as soon as he caught a whiff from the bowl he realized that he was eager to get some food into his stomach. He thanked the innkeeper courteously, and put the tray on a side-table. He dragged across a chair from the side of Viveka's bed, and settled himself down to eat. His hunger consumed him as he devoured the stew; it was only a matter of minutes before the food was all gone.

He looked around him as if in hope that the innkeeper would suddenly reappear with some more, but of course there was nobody. He concentrated his thoughts, and tried to mould them together in such a way as to conjure up the thin-eyed man, but all he succeeded in doing was turning the edges of his vision into a red fuzziness. He was on board the *Green Sceptre* again, its deck pitching and tossing, throwing him from side to side, and he was staggering in a clumsy dance. No, that was all wrong—of course he wasn't on the *Green Sceptre*; that had been long days ago. He was standing in the middle of an orchestra, surrounded by a hundred or more musicians, all of them staring at him expectantly, and he knew that he was expected to conduct them in a symphony, but he couldn't remember what the symphony was, or even if he'd ever heard it before, and he didn't care, so he threw his arms back and shrieked at the top of his voice as the hot vomit gushed down his chest, and all of a sudden he was a Zlanbeast, his great wings beating mercilessly against the feeble air, forcing it to succumb to his will.

He was staring at a threadbare carpet, the stink of his sick biting at his nostrils. He threw up again, adding to a lumpy puddle that extended around his hands and all the way to his knees. Someone had forced him to swallow hot coals, and now his stomach and his abdomen were smoulderingly burning away from within. He felt the pain of the glowing embers and asked himself quite lucidly whether or not he enjoyed it. On balance, he decided that he didn't.

Poison.

Now *there* was a new word, one that he hadn't encountered in a long while, and yet he greeted it like an old friend, while at the same time wondering why that old friend had chosen to visit unexpectedly after all this time.

Poison.

Now meeting an old friend who hadn't bothered to keep in touch over the years was one thing, but having to welcome him a second time was really a bit much.

Poison.

Even the most patient of us have our limits. This person was becoming arrogantly intrusive. Lone Wolf looked at him with active venom. This was no . . .

Poison.

. . . this was no friend, I was about to say before you interrupted me. No, correct that: *you're* no friend. You're just someone pretending that you knew me in the long ago, but now I recognize you for what you are. You're an . . .

Poison!

. . . imposter. Yes! May all the fiends of Helgedad devour you, you're nothing more than . . .

31

Poison!

Another convulsive heave of his shoulders, and he spat the last of the green vomit from him, rubbing the back of his hand over his mouth.

Viveka tried to poison me!

Somehow he got to his feet, and he stood there swaying, looking at the repulsive mess all around him.

No, it couldn't have been Viveka. Could it? When the innkeeper said my friend had sent supper up to me I assumed it was Viveka, but it could have been anyone.

He looked around him for a towel—anything to clear up the stinking pool of sickness. That seemed to be the wrong priority, he knew, but he carried on anyway. Perhaps Viveka had hung up a costume in the wardrobe that she didn't wear very often? Sure enough, there was soft cloth in his hands. First he wiped his face with it, using some of the stingingly cold water still left in the jug. Then he squatted down and did his best to clear up. The costume became clammy and heavy in his fist, and he realized that the task was hopeless. Always, back at the Kai Monastery, they'd said to him that he should tidy up after himself, but it looked as if for once he'd have to disobey instructions. A pity. And it had been such a nice carpet, too. Well, no, that was going a bit too far. In point of fact, now that he came to think of it, it had been a perfectly revolting carpet. It was definitely much improved by the transformation.

This thought cheered him as he remembered that there had been other things beside Viveka's costume in the wardrobe. Long, heavy, metallic things. Hmm. In fact, hadn't one of them been a sword, not unlike the sword which those fishermen had stolen from him?

Hmm. It definitely seemed to be a sword. He cut his thumb on the long blade of it, and grinned as he persuaded his mind to heal the tiny wound. He put the weapon in his belt, staggering with the effort, and decided that, right now, he was fit enough to conquer the whole of Aon—Aon and the Gods, if it came to that. Strong as

32

a . . . strong as a . . . His imagination failed him, but he concluded that he was very strong indeed.

The first time he went to the door it dodged to one side so that he walked into the wall.

On his second attempt the door must have realized that there was something serious afoot, because it stayed where it was and allowed him to open it.

The narrow stairs twisted like a tormented snake beneath his feet as he descended them. At their foot he met the one-eyed innkeeper, who gaped at his bedraggled appearance and recoiled to let him pass. Looking through reddened eyes Lone Wolf located the door into the taproom and staggered towards it. He clutched its jamb wildly, and surveyed the room beyond.

His travelling companions were seated at a large oak table, talking animatedly over the remains of their meal. Ganon was the first to notice him, and gave him a grin, which abruptly vanished when he saw the filth covering Lone Wolf's chest, not to mention the long gleaming sword which the youth somewhat waveringly held out before him.

Ganon jumped to his feet and came towards him.

"Whatever's happened? You look dreadful."

"Poison. Someone's tried to poison me."

There was an immediate commotion. An isolated part of Lone Wolf's mind dispassionately observed the reactions of the travellers—Viveka looking furious with herself, Halvorc mystified and disbelieving, Ganon and Dorier both concerned and enraged, and Parsion . . . Parsion looked horrified to see him.

Which was only to be expected. When the horses had bolted, out on the road, only three people could have set them off—Ganon, Dorier and the priest. But since then Lone Wolf had heard the two brothers state quite clearly that, as far as they knew, the whole affair had just been a dreadful accident; and, as Knights of Durenor, they were sworn to tell the truth.

Which left Parsion.

The priest observed Lone Wolf reaching this conclusion, and his face twisted. He leapt to his feet and turned towards a small door at the rear of the room. Viveka grabbed the sleeve of his robe and he hit out at her savagely, then unexpectedly drew a short black sword from his clothing. Lone Wolf recognized it immediately as a Giak blade, and the recognition gave strength to his right arm, so that he could bring the flat of his own weapon down with a smack on the chipped wooden table.

"You!" he spat.

"Yes, you Kai bratling, may Naar feast upon your soul." Parsion's sword moved like liquid, cutting Viveka across the right arm, severing the tendons on the inside of her elbow. She shouted in pain, but swiftly pulled a dagger from her belt using her other hand. Halvorc screamed, and the two Knights of the White Mountain were frozen, perplexity written large across their simple faces.

With the tip of his sword, Lone Wolf flipped an empty pewter platter directly up into the priest's face. Parsion ducked away, disconcerted by this unexpected move, and Viveka took the opportunity to jab her dagger into his belly; then, almost delicately, she fainted.

The priest was mortally wounded. He dropped his sword and clutched at the protruding handle of the dagger, staggering backwards to crash against the wall, shouting obscenities as Lone Wolf advanced vengefully, collapsing to sit with his back to the wall, a sudden spurt of blood fountaining from his mouth. Lone Wolf put the point of his sword against the wall next to the man's neck and leant against it, his forehead covered with oily sweat. He saw now, for the first time, the serpent tattoo on the priest's left wrist. He had seen that mark once before, back in Holmgard harbour, when he had been attacked in the Good Cheer Inn.

"Who are you, scum?"

"A better man than you'll ever be, whelp."

More blood issued from Parsion's mouth, but his face was still locked in a sneer of defiance.

"Who sent you?"

"No one."

"Then no one will mourn your dying."

Once more the blood gushed from the priest's mouth, spattering across the floor, flecking Lone Wolf's legs.

"And none will mourn yours, you little . . . "

The priest died, and there was a sudden racket behind Lone Wolf.

"Murder!" screamed the innkeeper. "They're murderers!"

"Wait!" said Ganon sternly. Lone Wolf turned exhaustedly to see what was happening. The two brothers drew their swords, and held them up against the innkeeper and half a dozen uniformed men. *The town guard*, thought Lone Wolf, dully. As he turned his attention back to the corpse of the priest, Viveka stirred on the floor, and her eyes flipped open to look up at him with cool alertness.

"You can keep the sword, little brother," she whispered. "You've earned it and you may well need it."

She winced painfully, then continued.

"There're horses out the back, there. Take one and go. These men'll string you up as a murderer."

"But—"

"I'll be all right. I've had worse wounds than this in my time. I'll catch you up if I can. Don't forget, I expect to collect a fee from your rich King Ulnar."

She smiled, and Lone Wolf realized that this was not the time to argue.

"You take care, big sister."

"Of course I will. Now, for Ishir's sake, get out of here."

She closed her eyes and, as far as Lone Wolf could see, drifted back into unconsciousness.

Swiftly, ignoring the shouting voices behind him, he searched the priest's blood-soaked garments. He found a half-empty vial, which he immediately deduced must have contained whatever foul tincture the priest had used to poison his food. He also found a crumpled roll of parchment, covered in the crude characters of written Giak. He could decipher only a few words—"Kai," "Port Bax," "Sommerswerd," "Vonotar." The rest of the writing must contain instructions, or perhaps just the details of his route from Ragadorn to Port Bax. The priest must have located him at the North Star Tavern and dogged him from there. But who had set the priest on him? And why?

The men of the town guard had summoned up enough courage to draw their swords and were now threatening the two Durenese knights. Lone Wolf had little time to waste trying to understand why the priest had tried to murder him. He mouthed a kiss towards Viveka's motionless face, and moved as swiftly as he could to the rear door, wishing that his arms and legs didn't feel so weak and that the room would stop its ceaseless rocking.

Out. Out into the coolness of the night. He found himself in a cobblestoned courtyard, aglow in the silver of the moon, which was nearing its full. Where were the horses that Viveka had talked about? There were only stables with sagging doors. The moon winked at him and he winked back, before the thought struck him that the moon doesn't wink. His sword—the sword that Viveka had given him—grazed the cobblestones, drawing sparks. He decided to sheathe the weapon and spent some seconds discovering that he didn't have a scabbard. He became petulant towards the Gods, who had failed to supply him with such a simple thing. A mere scabbard! Surely they could have managed that! No, what was he doing worrying about scabbards? He'd been sent out here to find horses, for some reason, some reason which he couldn't now exactly recall. Oh, yes, it was to escape from here—avoid the town guard and get away to Port Bax. That was what Viveka had told him to do, and Viveka was his elder sister, so she should know what was best for him.

He looked interestedly into the back of a haycart for some while, thinking how comfortable it would be to

36

snuggle himself down into the warm-smelling hay and sleep away the night. A small part of his faltering consciousness warned that this might be a very bad idea—but he couldn't remember why until a kaleidoscopic image of raised swords and angry faces tottered in front of his eyes. Aha! Being lynched! Yes, that was something he definitely didn't want to happen to him, although he couldn't for the moment remember quite why the experience would be so unpleasant. Now that he looked more closely at the hay, he began to associate the front ends of haycarts with animals of some kind, large animals with four legs and . . .

Horses!

That was it. Viveka had told him to take a horse.

He lurched around to the front of the cart and found not just one but two horses, both of which eyed him nervously. One of them was white and the other was black, but otherwise he couldn't tell any difference between them. He opted for the black one solely on the grounds that it was nearer to him, and cut its traces inexpertly with his sword. The beast stood quite still as he hauled his unwilling body up on its back.

He kicked with his heels, and the horse began resignedly to move. Behind him he sensed a sudden glow of light as the rear door of the Forlorn Hope opened, and the men of the town guard stumbled out into the courtyard, bumping into each other as their eyes adjusted to the dimness. He kicked the horse again, and it neighed in protest, but began to gallop along the deserted main street of Gorn Cove.

He fell forward across the animal's neck and allowed it to choose its own route. It swayed from side to side, negotiating the corners of the winding street with practised ease, clopping over the wooden bridge that spanned the slow-moving waterway known as Rat Creek, plunging eagerly up a steep hillside until they were at the very top of a cliff. Lone Wolf raised his head long enough to see, in the cold light of the moon, a signpost which told him that

Port Bax lay another fifty miles to his right. He nudged the horse in that direction, and it responded easily, its hooves beating the dried-mud road rhythmically.

He faded in and out of consciousness, sometimes feeling brightly alert and at other times revelling in a distorted reality which he knew, even as he experienced it, must be the product of dreams. The moon set, its silvery light now seeming somehow miserable, and the horse galloped on beneath him. The stars paled in the sky, which itself was turning from inkiness to a mellow grey-green colour.

He pulled himself erect on the horse's back and realized that the poison was at last leaving his system. He still felt divorced from what he saw all around him, and his limbs were infuriatingly slow to obey any of the commands he gave them, but his head had at last regained clarity. In the moist light of the dawning day he saw that he had left the barrenness of the Wildlands behind him. The horse was now trotting tidily along a road surrounded by sullen moors and waterlogged fens. A smudge ran along the horizon, far away to his right and then curving around ahead of him, and he guessed that this must be the Durenor forest, which served as the natural boundary between the two countries. It seemed that at last he was in sight of his destination.

He patted his horse on its right shoulder, and gratefully the big black animal eased itself to a halt. It began to graze on some of the grasses by the side of the road, and that reminded Lone Wolf that there was a great vacant space where his stomach should be. Of course, he hadn't brought any food with him, but he recognized some of the plants on the moor as edible, and he made a rather patchy, sour-tasting breakfast out of them. Then he climbed back on the horse's broad back and slapped the animal into a brisk trot.

An hour later he came to a fork in the road and, following his instincts, turned left. The day promised to be a beautiful one and, despite his ordeal, he found himself singing easily as the horse followed the road along the top of a high, grassy ridge. At the back of his mind there was concern about what might have happened to Viveka, but he kept his doubts firmly in place, assuring himself that she was almost certainly correct in her assessment that she would somehow come on through. From time to time he turned to scrutinize the road behind him, wondering if he might see her following him, but always the road was empty.

He went through the outskirts of a village, being treated to a good-natured hail of stones and clods of earth hurled by a gaggle of Szall children, and then left it behind as the road descended into a deep valley. The coarse brownish-green grasses of the moorland gave way to richer land, divided up into neatly tended fields. On the far side of the valley he could see the fringes of the Durenor forest, while off to his left tall cliffs jutted against the skyline. A smile appeared on his lips, although it was half an hour or so before he noticed that it had. He allowed the horse to amble on at its own pace, enjoying the feeling of the sunlight on his shoulders.

Very soon now he would be in Durenor. Presumably in that gruffly honest country he would find little difficulty in hiring transport to take him from Port Bax to the capital, Hammerdal, where he could claim the Sommerswerd for the salvation of his native country. There, too, he must ask if anyone knew the meaning of the name "Vonotar," which had been written on the scrap of parchment he had salvaged from the dead priest's clothing.

He waved cheerfully at a peasant girl working in one of the brown fields, and she straightened up from her labours and waved back. He grinned like a child, and started to sing again.

Soon, soon he would be in Durenor . . .

2

PORT BAX

1

He was passing through a little clump of trees when he heard cries of despair.

He halted the horse and twisted round, trying to work out where the sound had come from.

Yes—another scream. The high-pitched wail of a man in agony. Also other sounds—excited shriekings, like Giak cries. Over there, somewhere, to his right.

He slapped his horse on the rump and urged it forwards through a tangle of branches that slashed at his face. He felt for his sword.

Suddenly he was in the open. In a small clearing in front of him half a dozen Szalls were jumping and leaping in panic, shrilling to each other excitedly and pointing at the ground between them. There lay two bodies. One, dressed in the uniform of a Knight of the White Mountain, was clearly dead, his throat slashed wide open. The other, though, was very much alive; he was writhing in agony, screaming as he attempted desperately to drag from his chest the long carved spear which had impaled him. His eyes strained in his skull

41

as he looked towards Lone Wolf, wordlessly begging for help.

Lone Wolf pulled his sword free from his belt and kicked his horse towards the Szalls. They took one look at him and, wailing in terror, melted clumsily away into the undergrowth. He considered following them but realized that his duty lay here, with the injured man.

There's something wrong here, he worried as he clambered down off the back of his horse. *Something very wrong indeed. Szalls never attack human beings; they're too cowardly for that. For them to take on two strong men, one of them a knight . . . There's more here than meets the eye.*

He shivered uneasily and looked around the clearing, half-expecting to see hooded eyes watching him from the shelter of the trees. He could see nothing, but that did little to reassure him. Moving very warily, he checked the body of the knight to make sure that the man was indeed dead and then turned to the wounded person.

The man—a peasant, to judge by his clothing—had stopped screaming now. His exertions seemed to have drained him of all his strength, and he hardly moved as Lone Wolf knelt beside him. The spear had bitten cleanly into him, so that there was very little blood around the wound. Lone Wolf observed this with foreboding: the chances were that, as he removed the spear, he would unplug an artery and unleash a torrent of blood. He gathered some leaves and grass and tore a few strips from the peasant's clothing, ready to staunch any sudden flow. He muttered a few words of comfort as he clasped his hands around the shaft of the spear.

To his surprise, he found the weapon was made of metal, not wood, as he had assumed—although it was as light as a wooden spear. The shaft was covered with runes and other carved symbols, and Lone Wolf shivered again; he felt sure that there was magic at work here, and

42

he had a warrior's distrust of magic.

With his collection of cloth and foliage poised ready to stem the blood, he pulled the spear out of the man's chest in one smooth movement.

The peasant gave a long sigh of relief, which startled Lone Wolf. But he had other things on his mind. He clamped his fistful of cloth over the wound, throwing the spear away behind him.

Still no blood seemed to be flowing. Lone Wolf couldn't believe it. Cautiously he lifted away his make-shift bandage and looked at the peasant's chest.

The man chuckled, and then a bright, burning pain arced through Lone Wolf's head.

He staggered backwards, clutching his ears, and fell down abruptly on the knotted grass.

His eyes were filled with hot tears, yet he was able to see that the man who had seemed only moments before to be mortally wounded was now leaping agilely to his feet. Moreover, he was changing. The skin of his face was writhing and altering its hue, growing darker and shrinking as it seemed to decay, fitting itself closer and more tightly about his skull. His eyes were now burning with a bright red glow, and long fangs sprang up from his lower jaw.

A Helghast!

The spear—where had he thrown it?—must indeed be wrought of magic, for somehow it had frozen this vile creature's superhuman physical powers, threatening its very existence. And he, Lone Wolf, had like a credulous fool removed this demon's bane! No wonder the Szalls had been so full of terror. They must have come across this loathsome being in combat with the Knight of the White Mountains and realized that, whichever of the two combatants triumphed, they would be blamed and punished.

The pain in his mind was making it difficult for him to think. The Helghast must be using every ounce of its psychological abilities to attack him. How had the knight, whose mind had no defences against mental attack, ever survived this onslaught?

Sudden understanding filled Lone Wolf.

The spear . . . that must be the answer.

Howling without knowing that he was doing so, he crawled backwards, groping with his hands for the discarded weapon.

The Helghast stood above him, swaying, ready to attack.

Lone Wolf struck at its ankles with his sword, feeling the blade cut into the spawn-flesh. He couldn't see what was going on, though, and the shock of the impact made him lose his grip on his sword. The Helghast growled angrily. Orange and red suffused lights chased each other across Lone Wolf's eyes. The forest itself seemed to be stalking malevolently towards him. He retreated still further.

At last, the feel of metal against his fingers.

Immediately the pain receded from his brain, leaving only a numbing echo of its presence.

The Helghast yelled in fury as it saw that he had found the weapon, and sprang at him.

Lone Wolf rolled over, barely in control of his body's movements, and saw the creature's great clawed hands gouging out grooves of turf where he had lain only a moment before.

He forced himself to his knees and stabbed out blindly with the spear. He rapped the Helghast sharply on its side, but that was all.

It turned, on all fours, and stared at him with its infernal red eyes. Its lips were pulled well back from its fangs, and it drooled eagerly.

"Kill!" it barked gruffly, ready to spring. The words were rough around the edges, as if the creature had difficulty in mouthing them. "Kill in the name of Vono—"

The point of the spear cut deep into its cheek. Lone Wolf twisted the shaft, hoping to inflict a more serious wound, but the Helghast snapped its head away.

Lone Wolf rolled backwards, holding the spear out horizontally to one side, and found his feet. He lurched slightly, gaining his balance. His mind was racing now, filled with a savagery almost as debased as that of the Helghast. He rolled his lips and found that he, too, was slavering at the mouth.

A meaningless, harsh noise ripped itself from his throat. He swished the spear from side to side, moving it from one hand to the other, his eyes intent on the striated face of this spawn of Helgedad. He was conscious of no emotion save his need to kill. He wanted to destroy the beast utterly, to tear it into tiny shreds and scatter them all over the countryside, so that the pieces would be as far-flung as possible and, even in death, could never be reunited.

The Helghast was on its feet once more, and moving towards him cautiously, its huge armoured hands swinging by its sides. Lone Wolf jabbed the spear into its groin, withdrawing it every bit as swiftly.

The injury hardly interrupted the Helghast's advance.

"Kill," it growled, the words even more furred now that the flap of its cheek was dangling loose. "I kill Lone Wolf—die slow."

The spear took it in the right wrist. Again Lone Wolf twisted the shaft, and this time was rewarded by the sullen sound of splintering bones.

The Helghast screamed in astonished pain, staring at its hand dumbfoundedly.

The spear! thought Lone Wolf deliriously. *No normal weapon could harm a Helghast so readily! The beast can't understand why it's being injured so terribly!*

He swung the spear almost as if it were a sword, so that its razor-sharp tip raked across the Helghast's eyes. There was an eruption of ichor as one exploded over the carpet of grass, and the beast screamed yet again. It staggered to its knees, then fell forwards, its colossal hands scrabbling towards Lone Wolf's ankles.

"I kill!" it roared in anguish.

Lone Wolf stabbed straight forwards. The spear-point was deflected by the Helghast's skull. The jar of the collision shot up his arms. He danced lightly away from the creature's beckoning hands and cursed in silent pain.

The next time he drove forwards with the spear he felt the point push straight in through the Helghast's ear. The feeling, as the spear plunged relentlessly into the spongy mass that served the creature as a brain, was as if he were slicing into softened soap.

The Helghast gave a deafening scream. With shocking abruptness, it died.

As Lone Wolf watched, the creature's form faded from his vision, still frozen in its death-agony, in a half-crouch, its hands partly upraised towards its violated head. A purple-streaked wind seemed to swirl around Lone Wolf's head as the Helghast's image ebbed into nothingness.

He was left leaning against the moulded spear, his muscles aching, looking at an empty clearing where the signs of battle were all too evident.

He retrieved the sword that Viveka had given him and took a dagger from the belt of the dead knight, mumbling a few pointless excuses to the corpse as he did so. Then, very reluctantly, he turned to examine the pack left behind by the dead Helghast.

The first thing he drew from the pack was a black-bladed knife, its hilt etched with unfamiliar symbols whose meaning he couldn't decipher. As soon as Lone Wolf set eyes on it, he knew he was in the presence of Evil. Another, more mysterious, item was a block of cold obsidian. He turned it over in his hands, looking at it in bafflement. It seemed to have no conceivable purpose, yet its surface, too, was covered with those macabre symbols.

He reached further into the dark maw of the sack, pushing his hand gingerly forwards. His fingers touched

46

what seemed to be a roll of parchment, and he tugged it out into the light.

He half-gaged as he realized that this was no parchment. Although it was a scroll containing writing, it was made of uncured skin; and from the down on the skin he had little difficulty in identifying it as human—that of a young man or woman. His hands were trembling as he unrolled it to see what was written on it.

As with the parchment he had discovered among Parsion's clothing, this was written in the crudely formed Giak script, and he could make out only a few words. The one that leapt out at him was "Kai."

And the Helghast knew me by name! This was no chance encounter. Someone has been following my every step, and attempting to put an end to me. He squinted up at the sky, for a moment half-expecting to see the flying figure of the ancient man, but there was nothing to be seen. He peered at the script again, and suddenly another word leapt to his eye: "Vonotar."

Lone Wolf's mind raced. "Vonotar." That name had also appeared on Parsion's scroll. And the Helghast had used a word beginning "Vono." Surely the two must be the same!

It can't be coincidence. All of these attacks on me must have been orchestrated by some agent of the Darklords . . . the ancient man . . . Vonotar?

He thumbed through his memories. Where might he have heard the name before? Something told him that if only he could identify this Vonotar he would be far less vulnerable to the assaults on his life. But who could he ask? Banedon's "friend" Alyss? He wasn't certain that he really believed that Alyss existed. King Ulnar? Yes, the king might know, but he was many hundreds of miles away—still defending, Lone Wolf hoped, Sommerlund's capital from the greedy jaws of Zagarna's hordes.

All of a sudden he began wishing very much indeed that Viveka were with him. He had seen her ruthlessness and potential for cruelty, and he knew full well that she would kill him with hardly a thought if someone offered her enough money to do the job, but he found her, as it were, honest in her deviousness, and he felt sure that she would have been able to tell him more about this Vonotar. She had known—or deduced—far more about him than he would have believed possible, and he suspected that she knew more about the progress of the war as a whole than even he himself did. Moving among the low-lifers in the half-world in which she carried out her trade, she must hear unnumbered snippets of information—unguarded words spoken in taverns, or the empty-headed boasts of those who employed her skills.

The horse was gone. At some stage during his struggle with the Helghast Lone Wolf had sensed that something had disappeared from the clearing, so he was only slightly surprised to find it missing. Either it had fled from the scene of death or the Szalls had recognized it for the prime piece of horseflesh that it was and coaxed it away while his mind was taken up with other, more urgent things.

He wished it well—and found himself smiling in the sunlight. The animal had given him good service; even if it had deserted him he bore it no ill-will. He had travelled all the way from the Monastery to the Alema Bridge on foot, so the last few miles into Durenor and Port Bax should give him no trouble.

He tucked the sword and dagger into his belt, put the spear on his shoulder, and began to make his way back to the road.

2

Once again Qinefer was dreaming, and once again she was in Alyss's tent, but this time Alyss herself wasn't there. There was only the table, with a steaming cupful of adgana brew placed directly in its centre. Qinefer shyly reached out her hand for the cup but then hastily withdrew it; even although she was fully conscious that this was only a dream, she had no wish to risk even the slightest chance of becoming enslaved by the stuff.

She settled herself down in the other chair and waited impatiently for Alyss to make an appearance. She drummed her fingers on her knee, trying to force her thoughts to concentrate on anything else but the fact that she found waiting boring. She was conscious of the fact that, in some way which she didn't as yet fully understand, Alyss was vitally important to the resistance against the invasion of Zagarna and his spawn-bred hosts, but at the same time she found the sprite-like woman profoundly irritating. Besides, Alyss was very definitely magic; Qinefer tried to persuade herself that she kept an open mind about magic, but deep down inside herself she distrusted and disliked it.

How dare she keep me waiting like this? Am I not among the foremost of all King Ulnar's Knights of the Realm?

She smiled at her own arrogance. Only a few days ago she had been nothing but a humble farmer's daughter; now she was taking airs and graces to herself. She still felt as if she were the same person—despite her tally of dead Giaks and other spawn, notably (she preened herself) a Helghast and two Gourgaz—yet still there was a part of her that felt as if Alyss's lateness was nothing more than rank impertinence.

Time passed very slowly for Qinefer. She pushed her dream-fingers through her dream-hair, tidying it abstractedly, realizing as she did so that the effort was wasted, was nothing more than a way of making the leaden seconds pass by a little more quickly. She took the cup of adgana—this time there was no temptation to swig it back—and used the surface of the liquid as a mirror in which to check her appearance: she was pleased to note that, in this dream-state, the unsightly scab on her nose had disappeared. But there was a limit to the number of things she could do here in Alyss's tent, and when she went to its door to look out there was nothing to see, as she pushed the flaps aside, but a bleak moonlit desert, an eternity of sand stretching away in every direction.

She returned to her chair, humming frustratedly through her teeth. *Is this going to be one of those dreams where nothing happens the whole night long? I could be discovering new continents, or perhaps taming wild animals . . .*

Where Alyss had been seated in Qinefer's earlier dream there was now a coalescence of the air. She watched with a sort of half-hearted fascination as drifts of various textures came together, knitting themselves, until they formed the hazy figure of an incredibly ancient man. His face was covered in the furrows of antiquity; the ridges of his eyebrows, over the hot flare of his eyes, reminded her in some way of birds' wings. He was dressed in a robe of faded blue, decorated with stars which had once been silver but which had now tarnished to show the muted grey of pewter. His hands were like the claws of a lobster as they scuttled across the surface of the table.

"Welcome to my establishment," said the ancient man.

Qinefer rose to her feet and spat at him.

"I recognize you!" she snapped. "You're that—"

The wizened man held up a frail hand to deflect her words.

"Yes, yes, I know. You have little cause to love me. I'm Vonotar, the symbol of everything you hate. Yet I think you ought to listen to me a little while longer, young lass."

"Why should I?"

"Why should you indeed? Because I can tell you of a way in which you can become the foremost warrior in all Magnamund."

Qinefer stared at him with unabated hatred.

"Oh, yes, you can forget about that fool of a youth, Lone Wolf. If he's not dead already he will be soon. And good riddance, if you ask me, good riddance." The

50

magician's eyes briefly flared into blueness. "But you—you, my dear—you could have in your arms the strength of all the magic I can bring to bear. There would be few, if any, who could stand against you. Soon you could be the ruler of all Sommerlund, the armies of King Ulnar under your sole command. He, of course, you would have to . . . dispose of"—the magician's lips arched fastidiously—"but I'm sure that would be a simple enough task for you, knowing that the prize would be your own supremacy."

"I curse your grave," hissed Qinefer.

"A typical reaction of the emotionally immature, if I may be so bold as to say so," piped Vonotar querulously, damning the agedness that coloured his voice. "But think about it a little longer, young woman. Just think about it."

He nudged the cupful of adgana towards her, and with a *flwhup!* of imploding air, disappeared from her sight. She looked at the place where he had been, and started to grin.

I think you've made a big mistake, she thought.

3

Lone Wolf came to the crest of a hill and saw the vast gloominess of the Durenor forest spread out ahead of him. The stern-looking trees were a dark coniferous green; between their erect, parallel trunks it seemed as if they had captured an ocean of cool dusk. Lone Wolf smiled. Ever since childhood he had been drawn to forest places. The sight of this great expanse made him feel as if he were coming home.

Where the road entered the trees a large wooden guard-tower had been erected—many decades ago, to judge by its ramshackle appearance. From this distance Lone Wolf could just make out the silhouette of a sentinel in position on the upper level of the structure.

He began to jog easily down the road, still grinning to himself.

The guard must have seen him early on, because by the time Lone Wolf was within about twenty yards of the dilapidated wooden tower the man was emerging from its base, holding a spear at the ready. He was dressed in the red coat of a Durenese man-at-arms, and to Lone Wolf this was a gleeful proclamation that, despite all the hazards of the past few days, he had at last succeeded in reaching the border between Durenor and the Wildlands.

"Well met, friend," he cried, easing his pace.

The sentinel kept his spear defensively pointing forwards, but half-smiled.

"Who are you, and what is your business?" he said formally.

Lone Wolf was uncertain what to reply. He'd become so used to using subterfuge recently that it was now almost like second nature to him. On the other hand, Durenor was an historic ally of Sommerlund . . . He decided to opt for honesty, and gave the soldier the bare bones of his mission, carefully playing down its importance just in case he might have been unlucky enough to have found a traitor among the Durenese ranks. Also in his mind was his recent encounter with the Helghast; he was uneasily conscious that every human being to whom he spoke, no matter what his or her appearance, might prove to be another of the Darklords' spawn.

As he spoke the sentry's spear lowered. When Lone Wolf had finished his terse explanation the man said: "Have you some proof of this?"

Wordlessly Lone Wolf held out his right hand. On its middle finger was the Seal of Hammerdal. The soldier recognized it at once, and his mouth dropped open.

"I had no wish to see that in my lifetime," he said sadly. "When a Sommlending bears the Seal of Hammerdal to Durenor it can mean only one thing—war."

"I told you. We're already at war."

"Yes, you Sommlending are. But we Durenese have known peace for many long years now."

"If Zagarna succeeds in conquering Sommerlund, his armies will spread to other nations. Durenor is sure to be among the first. Better to attack him now than to suffer the wrath of his invasion later."

"You're probably right," said the sentry with a shrug, "but I wish that you weren't—indeed, that you weren't even here. I've a wife and children. I'd hoped they could live out their lives in peace." He pulled himself upright. "Still, enough of that. Obviously you must pass. I'd come with you to guide you, but I'm alone here 'til sunset. If you'd like to wait that long . . . ?"

"No," Lone Wolf said decisively. "I've already taken much longer on my journey than I'd intended. I've got to press ahead."

"Then good speed," said the sentry, almost gratefully. "It's not many miles from here to Port Bax."

The man turned and pointed along the road into the forest.

"Keep on this way until you come to a stunted oak tree. It's very recognizable—you can't miss it. The road forks there. Both roads will take you to Port Bax, but the one on the left is the quicker."

"Thank you," said Lone Wolf, "and may Kai be with you in the troubled times to come."

"And also with you," responded the soldier automatically. Then he sucked in his breath expressively. "Aye, and I mean that, young man. It's for all of us to fight Evil. I just wish this hadn't happened in my time."

Lone Wolf touched palms with him briefly, and then headed off down the road, alternately jogging and walking, making good speed between the trees. The forest all around him was eerily still: no birds sang in the treetops; no wind stirred the branches. After a while, however, he could hear a distant sound ahead of him.

It wasn't long before he discovered what it was. The forest opened in a sudden rush of light, and ahead he could see a long, graceful bridge of white stone. The sound was the chopping, argumentative movement of the waves of a great tract of water, which extended away from him on both sides as far as he could see. He recognized it as the Rymerift, a great geological gash, in places two miles wide, which separated the bulk of Durenor from the continental mainland, and joined the Gulf of Durenor to the Kuri Sea. Its waters were said to be as much as a mile deep.

Here the Rymerift was only a few hundred yards wide, but still Lone Wolf marvelled at the construction of the bridge. Although it was broad enough to carry only a single wagon, it had been built with great care and craftsmanship. As he ran his fingers along the ancient stone parapet, he admired the artistry of the stonemasons. Every boulder had been laboriously carved so that it exactly matched those on either side. Set into the stones, every few tens of yards, was a sculpted head representing some symbol of Durenor's glory and pride. The years and the damp saltiness of the air over the waters of the Rymerift had etched and pocked these, but still Lone Wolf could appreciate the brilliance that had gone into their creation.

On the far side of the bridge there was a reassuring signpost:

PORT BAX—3 MILES

He grinned at it happily: he should be there in less than an hour.

In fact, the sign-maker had been a little optimistic, for it was nearly dusk by the time Lone Wolf caught his first sight of Port Bax.

He stopped. The only places of any size that he had seen before were Holmgard and Ragadorn, but neither of them—certainly not the latter—could match this place for beauty. A curve of gentle hills surrounded the city on three sides; on the fourth was the Gulf of Durenor.

The soft evening light picked out the faded pink of the stone used to build most of the houses and other buildings, including the tall, superbly proportioned castle that crowned the largest of the ring of hills. On the far side of the city Lone Wolf could just discern the harbour area, where a number of large war-galleons moved easily at their moorings.

He made his way down to the city and found, to his initial astonishment, that the entrance was unguarded. Then he realized that, of course, Durenor was not at war, and so there was no reason why the city walls should be extensively patrolled. During his few days in Sommerlund since the start of the war he had become totally acclimatized to the way that every habitation or dwelling-place was rigorously defended. He seemed to have spent half a lifetime living in a state of emergency.

As it was the time of the evening meal, there were comparatively few people in the streets. Lone Wolf made his way in the general direction of the harbour, on the supposition that the Sommerlund consulate would probably be near the water. He stopped a young couple to ask them for directions, but they were unable to help, although they smiled in friendly fashion at what was, to them, his thick Sommlending accent.

As he was leaving them, the woman turned back towards him.

"Ask in the city hall," she said kindly. "They're bound to be able to tell you there."

She pointed to the other side of the road, where a tree-lined avenue led off.

"It's just up there," she added. "On the right."

A couple of minutes later Lone Wolf was standing in front of a large building surmounted by a copper-coloured dome. He climbed a broad flight of stone steps and was greeted by a brass plaque which confirmed that this was, indeed, the city hall. A welcoming splash of

55

warm light spilled from its half-open doors, and Lone Wolf, without hesitation, entered.

Just inside, an old man with a long beard was studying a huge leather-bound book that rested on a lectern before him. Lone Wolf started, remembering the ancient man he had seen in the skies, but almost immediately he relaxed again, because the scholar was eyeing him with a genial look of genuine interest and amiability.

"Are you looking for someone, young man?" he asked courteously, his tones deep and grave.

Lone Wolf explained what he wanted, and the scholar looked somewhat surprised.

"It's not hard to find the consulate," he said, his fingers working at the straggly ends of his beard, "but it's not easy to get there."

Lone Wolf looked baffled. Was the man speaking in riddles?

The scholar saw his confusion and smiled again.

"The consulate's in the naval quadrant, you see," he explained, "and that's a restricted area. You'll need to get a red pass before they'll let you in."

"How do I go about that?"

"You can get a pass from the Captain of the Port Watchtower, although I doubt that he'll see you tonight. You'd be better off waiting 'til morning. There are plenty of inns where you can spend the night."

"But I've got to get to the consulate as soon as possible. It's urgent."

The old man shrugged sceptically, and his eyes on Lone Wolf were shrewd.

"Well, you can try," he said reluctantly. "The Port Watchtower is close by here. Turn right as you leave the building and keep walking until you reach the end of the avenue and you'll see it in front of you. To get from there to the consulate you'll need to get into the naval quadrant by the Red Gate."

He gave Lone Wolf a few further directions and then wished him good speed.

The Port Watchtower was even closer than Lone Wolf had anticipated. It was a tall white building, fronted by a rickety-looking set of rusting metal steps. Wearily he climbed these, knowing that the handrail was smearing him with a red-brown stain but past the stage of caring for such trivia—anyway, his tunic was already so badly stained that a few extra marks would hardly make any difference. At the top of the steps he paused and looked around him. Off to his right there was a short cobbled street and at the end, just as the old scholar had described, there was a high stone wall with a red gate set in it. Two soldiers were standing guard; their red uniforms looked black in the dim light. Lone Wolf could see, over the top of the wall, the masts of some of the larger ships moored in the harbour. His nostrils flared eagerly, and a new strength came to him. At last he was coming close to his destination. Surely they would send an escort with him from the consulate to Hammerdal.

The main door of the Port Watchtower was ancient and unprepossessing, slumping sorrowfully on its hinges. He knocked on it, and was hardly surprised when there was no reply; it looked like the sort of door which would admit people only with the greatest reluctance. As he manipulated its greasy metal handle and pushed it open, it squealed disappointedly, making it plain to him that, as far as it was concerned, he was an intruder.

He found himself in a large, badly lit hall. With some difficulty he made out the sign on a door near to him:

NAVAL QUADRANT RED PASSES

He rapped on it, and again there was no reply—perhaps it wasn't the Durenese custom to respond when people knocked on their doors? In fact, it suddenly came to him, for the last few hours he had been assuming, without really thinking about it, that the Durenese were like the Sommlending in all respects, just because they looked very similar, spoke a language that was so closely related to the Sommlending tongue that they were barely more than dialects of each other, and were of course Sommerlund's staunchest allies. But the assumption wasn't a rational one. There was so much that he didn't know about Durenese society and customs that, if he wasn't careful, he could easily find himself in trouble through sheer ignorance. He could make a perfectly innocent remark to someone and unwittingly cause them considerable offence.

However, he couldn't stand dithering here any longer. He pushed the door open confidently and stepped through it into a room whose sole unifying factor was absolute chaos. Piles of documents, ledgers and curling sheets of paper lay everywhere, across desks, along shelves and all over the floor. Charts had been pinned all over the walls, and most of them were drooping and peeling gracelessly. The air was thick with the smell of tobacco smoke and the simple odour of constant human habitation; clearly it had been weeks since last the window had been opened. A naked lamp flickered—dangerously, Lone Wolf thought, in view of the amount of loose paper around—and in its light he could see a middle-aged, rather raddled-looking man in gaudy naval uniform working away busily with a quill pen at a thick battered ledger. The only sounds were the scratch of the quill and the *puttaputta* of the lamp.

The naval officer continued writing, his face close to the paper of the ledger, his eyes peering myopically at the words; those eyes were a strikingly pale, almost metallic-seeming blue, and they watered from the intensity of the effort. The man's lips moved silently as he worked.

Lone Wolf coughed artificially.

No reaction.

He coughed again.

The officer looked up, his eyes refocusing slowly, and at last registered Lone Wolf's presence.

"Ah, you'll be the messenger sent by Admiral Simey. Bit early, young lad, bit early you are. I've not finished

yet, so you'll just have to wait. Terrible thing, terrible."
His voice was prissily fussy. He shook his head wearily
and went back to work.

"I'm not a messenger. Well, not in the sense you think.
And I'm not from Admiral Simey."

"True, true," said the officer, clearly not listening. "But
once he looks at these figures there'll be heads rolling,
I can tell you. Soap! That's the problem, laddie—soap!
And I don't like the smell of it!"

"I . . . I . . . ah . . . "

"Corruption! Nothing but corruption! The world's full
of corruption these days, and most of it's to do with soap.
It fair gets me in a lather." He stared firmly at Lone Wolf.
"I hope you never get involved in soap, lad."

Lone Wolf had just been thinking that, with luck, he
would be able to take a bath when he reached the
consulate, and so he was startled—it was as if this man
had been reading his mind.

"But I—"

"Been using too much of it, the sailors have. More
than they could possibly use. My figures prove it." He
tapped the ledger in front of him proudly. Flecks of ink
sprayed from the quill over the paper, but he paid them
no heed. "Here's the damning evidence, I tell you! Our
sailors have been stealing the navy's soap by the crateful.
Doubtless selling it on the black market. Making an
absolute fortune, I'll be bound."

"That's not what I came about," said Lone Wolf.

"Isn't it? Then what in the name of the Darklords are
you doing here? Go away, and stop bothering me. Can't
you see I've got a lot of soap to calculate?"

"I need a red pass. I need to get to the Sommlending
consulate as swiftly as possible."

"Aha! A soap-smuggler, are you? I can imagine your
type! So that's where the stuff's all going, is it? To
Sommerlund? You should be ashamed of yourself, laddie. One so young as you to be corrupted by soap so
early."

The man grappled around him myopically.

"Dash and thunder," he muttered, "but I'm sure I had a sword here somewhere. How in the world am I going to slay you for the vile soap-smuggler you are if I can't find my sword anywhere? Look, lad, can *you* see it anywhere?"

The sword was propped up against the wall behind him, but Lone Wolf decided it would be best not to tell him this. The last thing he wanted to do was to waste time having an unnecessary fracas with this strange clerk.

"I don't know anything about soap," he said curtly. "All I want is a red pass."

"Deny it, would you? Adding perjury to your crimes, eh? I know I had that sword somewhere—and a fine sword it is, too. Given to me by my grandfather when he was a boy. No, wait a moment. It was me that was the boy. I say, could I borrow your sword for a moment?"

"Where's the Captain of the Port Watch? I have to get hold of a red pass—right now."

"The Captain of the Port Watch? Don't tell me that he's involved in the conspiracy, too? Well, I'd never have believed it. Mind you, I've noticed him smelling unusually perfumed from time to time. Sampling the merchandise, I've no doubt. And to think I was so foolish as never to suspect him?"

Lone Wolf began to wonder if all Durenese were like this. If so, he might as well turn and go home right now.

"Look," he half-wept, feeling the full effect of his exhaustion once again, "all I want to do is to see the Captain of the Port Watch to ask him for a red pass into the naval quadrant!"

"That's what they all say," said the officer suspiciously, ceasing his frenzied scrabbles for his sword and looking at Lone Wolf with a critical expression on his face.

"All who? I mean, who're 'they'?"

"Soap-smugglers, of course! They come in here several times a day, pretending that all they want is to apply for a red pass. But I've learned their little trick now."

"It says on the door that this is the place to get—"

"Yes, a cunning subterfuge of mine, wasn't it, putting that notice up?"

"Then perhaps you could tell me where I could get a—"

"I know what you're about to say! A red pass is what you want! Then why in the name of all that's holy, and a few of the unholy things, too, now that I come to think about it, didn't you say so in the first place?"

"I tried to." Lone Wolf leaned on his sword and stared at a mouse in the corner of the room. It was sitting half-upright, chewing at its paws. *I'd rather be talking to you than to this maniac*, he thought wearily in the direction of the mouse.

"Well, that's simple enough, if you really want one."

The officer was clearly still suspicious, but he looked at last to be cooperative.

Thank Ishir for that!

"Well, may I have one, please?"

"No. Of course not. I told you it was simple enough."

Lone Wolf felt for the dagger he'd acquired after fighting the Helghast. Frustration was building up inside him to the point where he was terrified that, in a sudden fury, he would stab this man through the heart.

"But," he said, spitting each word individually between his teeth, "my business is urgent. I can't be delayed any longer. If you can't give me a red pass yourself then for Kai's sake take me to the captain!"

"You're strangely convincing for a soap-smuggler. Even if you are genuine, laddie, you'd need to show me your access papers and some proof of authorization from your commanding officer. Also, there's King's Decree Number 17 (As Revised) to be taken into account. One of my favorite decrees, that."

"I don't *have* any papers!" Lone Wolf shouted. "I've come all the way here from Sommerlund on an important mission. I've risked my life a hundred times, and I'm not going to be stopped by some idiotic old dodderer whose . . . whose mind is full of soap!"

"Well, if you put it like that, all I can suggest you do is come back tomorrow. It's far too late at night to give you a red pass. You'd probably just lose it in the dark and have to come back for another."

Lone Wolf remembered his encounter with the sentry. What had worked once might well work again.

He pushed his hand forward across the officer's desk, pulling back his sleeve so that the Seal of Hammerdal could be clearly seen.

"Will that convince you," he hissed, "that I'm here on a matter of some importance?"

The clerk looked at it warily, then touched it inquisitively with his fingernails. "It's the real thing?" he said, his voice losing much of its pettiness. "Not an imitation made out of soap?"

"It's the real thing. It was given to me by King Ulnar himself."

"Ah."

Without another word the clerk pulled himself to his feet and led Lone Wolf out of the room. Occasionally tripping and stumbling through the gloom, he went along a corridor and up a flight of wooden stairs, then along another corridor that was even more poorly lit than the first. Finally he came to a halt at a blackened-oak door and knocked on it sharply.

"Yes!" came a bellowing voice from within.

Well, thought Lone Wolf, *that sorts out the problem of whether or not the Durenese answer when someone knocks on their doors.*

62

The clerk led him in. The room was huge—seemingly far too vast for the size of the building. At the far end was an imposing onyx desk behind which sat one of the tiniest men Lone Wolf had ever seen.

"Come on, you two," boomed the Captain of the Port Watch. "But I'll have your livers if you're here to waste my time."

The room echoed emptily as the two of them clattered across it to the captain's desk. Lone Wolf noted idly that it, like the rest of the room, was starkly bare. Its top seemed to have been freshly polished. It looked as if it would have been disgusted if anyone had presumed to place a piece of paper on it. The contrast with the clerk's office below was bizarre.

Lone Wolf didn't beat about the bush. He showed the Seal of Hammerdal immediately, and told the captain tersely about the war in Sommerlund; beside him the clerk punctuated his account with little squeaks and gasps.

As soon as Lone Wolf had finished, the Captain of the Port Watch looked at the clerk furiously. "You buffoon of a snivelling little apology for a Szall's giblets!" he snarled. "Why didn't you bring this man to me immediately?"

"Well, sir, you never know these days—"

"Go and make out a red pass at once! At the double! Quicker than that! Or so help me I'll—"

The clerk didn't stop to hear what the captain would do to him. Throwing the occasional terrified glance back over his shoulder, he fled rattlingly down the length of the room, looking desperately anxious to be out of his superior's presence. Lone Wolf tried not to grin; the man was almost whimpering in his distress.

"I don't know why we put up with him," said the captain reflectively, staring into the empty space where the clerical officer had been. "But every time I try to get Simey transferred to another division my dear fellow-officers think up so many good reasons why he should stay here that I . . . I just give up."

63

He rubbed his small but muscle-knotted hand across his forehead.

"Simey?" said Lone Wolf. "But he seemed at first to think I'd been sent by an admiral called Simey."

"Oh," said the captain sadly, "you've had the soap treatment, have you?"

"Well, in short, yes."

"Poor old Simey. For years now he's had the fantasy that a cousin of his is an admiral, and that this admiral is constantly asking him to check up on the usage of soap in the fleet—important economies could be made, you know the sort of thing. Simey's convinced that there's a colossal conspiracy afoot to rob the navy. To tell you the truth, though, I wonder what our men *do* do with the official-issue soap. You should smell a few of them. No—don't. Start by smelling just the one. More than a couple is a lethal dose."

Lone Wolf began to wonder if he were to be treated to another conversation like the one he had suffered in the clerk's office. Fortunately he was saved from any such possibility by the reappearance of the clerk himself. The man ran puffingly down the room and made as if to put the document he was clutching down on the captain's desk.

"Not there, you fool!"

The man recoiled, horrified by the sacrilege he had been about to commit.

"Give it to our young guest, and then get out of my sight—or I'll put you on a diet of soap for a fortnight!"

"Not that! Sir, you wouldn't—"

"Wouldn't I?" The captain stared wrathfully at his cowering underling. "Now, get out!"

As the clerk dashed away in terror, Lone Wolf heard him mutter under his breath, "So *that's* what he does with all the soap!"

"I thank you for your help," said Lone Wolf politely to the Captain of the Port Watch. "If you'll excuse me, however, I'd like to be on my way as soon as possible."

"Yes, you'll want to get to your consulate."

Moments later Lone Wolf was hurrying down the cobbled street to the Red Gate. The guards there inspected his pass, saluted smartly and allowed him through. On the other side of the wall he found himself in an open square lit by the tall beacons lining the quayside. On the far side of it he could see a building fronted by marble pillars above which the sun-flag of Sommerlund flapped lazily in the night breeze. He ran tiredly across the square, feeling his sword batting against his leg as he moved. Now that he was here, the accumulated tiredness of the past few days flowed into every limb of his body, so that he was stumbling as he hauled himself up the stone steps of the consulate.

Luckily the guards on duty at the door immediately recognized his Kai clothing, tattered and stained though it was, and they sprang forward to help him. Two of them supported him, his arms around their shoulders, while a third dashed off into the building. He returned within a few moments, accompanied by a distinguished-looking grey-haired man, who was dabbing at his lips with a table napkin.

He looked at Lone Wolf, and his casual interest turned to enthusiasm.

"A Kai! Thank all the beneficences of Ishir! I trust that you're the bearer of good news. We've heard rumours of the dreadful things that are said to be happening in Sommerlund. Look, let's not talk here. Come inside, come inside. You look all done in. Come and sit down in front of the fire and fortify yourself with some food and drink—and then tell us all your news."

4

Lone Wolf was conscious only of a blur of light and sound as the guards took him into the consulate. The next time that he was fully aware of his surroundings he was sitting on a comfortably quilted chair, his feet stretched out in front of him, a glass of spicy-smelling wine being thrust into his hand. As he looked around him he could see that his arrival had interrupted some sort of formal dinner party, for everyone else there was dressed fashionably. Platters still half-filled with food littered a long oak table. The room was lit by an array of sputtering candles set in silver candelabra that ran in a single line down the table's centre. Lone Wolf became very self-conscious about his filthy garb, and then settled himself more relaxedly into his chair. *If they'd been through what I've been through . . .*

There was one person there who wasn't dressed in fine silks and furs. This was a tall, bulky man clad in heavy chain mail and with a sword at his hip. Lone Wolf guessed his age to be no more than about thirty or so, and was surprised when this man gruffly introduced himself as Lord-Lieutenant Rhygar, King Ulnar's envoy to Durenor. Lone Wolf had somehow expected an older man.

Rhygar ignored the rest of the dinner guests and dragged a chair up to join Lone Wolf. He beckoned to a servant, and almost at once Lone Wolf found a platter being placed on his knee. Using his fingers, he picked up a thigh of plump chicken and began to gnaw at it greedily. Rhygar watched him with a sympathetic look in his eye, recognizing his eager hunger, and forbore to question him until the first of its pangs had been assuaged.

"Once you've finished that and rested for a few minutes, young Kai," he said, "we'll set you out a proper meal and you can tell me what's been happening in Sommerlund."

Lone Wolf finished the chicken and drank another couple of glasses of the sweet wine. He looked into the flames of the log fire, and began to feel his vision grow muzzy. All that he really wanted to do was sleep, but he knew that he must stay awake for an hour or two longer. He flexed the muscles of his arms and worked his shoulders in a rolling movement, forcing the sleepiness to recede from his body.

It was with a close approximation to an alert smile that he finally turned to Rhygar and said: "Well, where would you like me to begin?"

"At my dinner table," said the envoy. "I've never been averse to a second supper, myself, and I'm sure that my guests here"—he gestured around him—"will be happy enough to join us as we eat. We're all Sommlending, as you can see, so we've no need to worry about our loyalty to the cause."

Lone Wolf remembered the priest, Parsion. He, too, had been a Sommlending. However, Lone Wolf kept his doubts to himself.

The meal was splendid. Some of the foods Lone Wolf couldn't identify. He and Rhygar ate steadily and in silence for a while, the other guests making small talk among themselves, obviously eager to hear what the young Kai had come to tell them but at the same time too courteous to interrupt him as he ate.

Finally Lone Wolf leaned back in his chair and belched, covering his mouth with his hand to stifle the noise.

"That was good," he said sincerely. "I should eat here more often."

Rhygar laughed, and dutifully the others joined in.

"Now, friend," said the envoy, "tell us your news."

"There's little of it that's good," Lone Wolf began. He spoke for perhaps a quarter of an hour, grateful that at last he could tell his full story, missing out none of the details. From time to time Rhygar broke with a question, asking for clarification of this point or that, his attentive grey eyes fixed on Lone Wolf's face. He seemed especially interested in Ulnar's plans to defend the besieged Holmgard, and asked for particulars of troop dispositions and weaponry which Lone Wolf embarrassedly confessed that he just didn't know. Rhygar looked markedly impressed as the young Kai told him of some of the struggles he had had with his foes, and when he described Viveka the envoy began to smile, clearly recognizing her; otherwise his expression was as grave as the information warranted.

At the end of Lone Wolf's account Rhygar sat leaning forward over the table silently for a minute or more, staring at the oak surface, obviously deep in thought. Then he looked up.

"What you need is a lot of rest, my courageous young friend," he said, "and the ministrations of my personal physician. In the morning we'll set off for Hammerdal."

Lone Wolf was surprised. He hadn't expected the Lord-Lieutenant himself to accompany him, and he wasn't absolutely certain that he liked the idea. Still, at least it proved that here at last was someone who was taking his mission seriously. He'd grown tired of being fobbed off by one person after another who assumed that, just because of his youth, his quest could be of little importance.

A short while later Lone Wolf was in a luxurious bedroom. Rhygar's physician turned out to be a cheerful individual, about the same age as his master, and as he stripped Lone Wolf off and began to attend to those of his wounds which he hadn't been able to cure through the use of his own healing abilities, he kept up a steady flow of talk. Soon Lone Wolf began to realize that his escort for the journey to Hammerdal could hardly have been better chosen. From the physician's account it was plain that Rhygar's career had been an impressive one.

Rhygar, it emerged, had been born to a Sommlending father and a Durenese mother, and, so the physician said, had inherited all of the virtues of both nations and none of their vices. He had early shown himself to be a precocious military genius, and had rapidly been promoted within the Durenese army. Some years ago he had been put in command of a joint Durenese/Sommlending army which had successfully repelled an invasion of Ice Barbarians from the chilly wastelands of Kalte, to the north, and his heroism during that brief war had made him something of a legend in Durenor. He had been an obvious choice as King Ulnar's envoy to the country when the previous envoy had died, just two years ago. Rhygar, Lone Wolf gathered, was respected for his sagacity during peacetime as much as for his ferocity and mastery of strategy in war. The more the physician spoke about him, the more the man rose in Lone Wolf's estimation.

He was impressed by the physician, too. He noticed hardly a twinge of pain as his wounds were cleaned. He was ushered into a steamingly scented hot bath—*enough soap to satisfy even Simey*, he thought wryly—thoroughly washed, then pummelled dry with soft, fluffy towels. He was refreshed enough by all this to have the strength to cure some of the worst of the bruises and cuts which he had picked up along the way, and the physician watched with interest, then applied strange-smelling unguents and ointments to the remainder.

The physician helped him into a well used flannel nightgown that was considerably too large for him and settled him into a deliciously soft bed. Part of Lone Wolf's mind was humming with activity, with anticipation of the hazards that the morrow might possibly bring, but the rest of it was working at the most animal of levels, simply enjoying the feel of the warmth and softness of the pillows and bedclothes. He mustered enough self-control to raise his head as the physician blew out the candles.

"I thank you, Doctor."

"Think nothing of it," said the physician, standing in the door, framed by the orange-yellow light from the corridor beyond.

"G'night," said Lone Wolf, feeling the sleep washing over him.

"A pleasant journey on the morrow," said the physician.

Lone Wolf tried to make a polite response, but his exhaustion had finally conquered him.

3

TARNALIN

1

For three days, Lone Wolf had ridden with Rhygar and three of his most skilled fighting men. At nights they had made camp as late as possible, rising as soon as the earliest glimmers of dawn had stolen across the sky, pressing forwards urgently. In the evenings they had talked cheerfully together, and something of a competition had sprung up between them to decide who could recount the tallest convincing tale of his own heroic exploits. Sometimes Lone Wolf was uncomfortably aware that Rhygar might actually be telling the truth, so he took care not to get so carried away with the embroidering of his own yarns, that he came out with something the older warrior might know for a fact to be impossible. In the unsteady light of the campfires, Giaks and Ice Barbarians died in their thousands, most decapitated but a few consigned magically to the oblivion of Naar's desolate darkness. It was all stirring stuff, and Lone Wolf admired the others' inventiveness even as he told them, quite seriously, about how he had seized three Gourgaz by the scruffs of their necks and drowned them in a cauldron of beef broth.

He considered himself to be particularly effective when imitating the Gourgaz's plaintive cries for mercy as they had told him that they were vegetarians.

The road had wound roughly northwards, following the meandering course of the Durenon River. The river was sometimes sleepy, moving massively and slowly; at other times it raced between narrow cliffs of reddish rock.

Lone Wolf was the first to wake that morning, and he was enjoying the solitude. He had washed himself in a stream, and was feeling clean and alert. His ears were filled by the sound of crashing water; near where they had camped the night before, the Durenon spilled itself over a great wall, well over a hundred feet high, to cascade into angry pools beneath. He sat beside the dead black branches of last night's fire, appreciating the sound of the cascade and the sight of the Hammerdal mountains, behind whose snow-capped peaks, he knew, lay the capital of Durenor, Hammerdal itself. His mind ran back to the first and only time he had seen the Durncrags— the savage range of mountains that divided Sommerlund from the Darklands—and he was amused by the difference in his reaction. The Hammerdals seemed like friends to him, representing a safe cordon about the capital city of Durenor, whereas the Durncrags had, from the moment he'd first seen them, stood like foes against the skyline.

Rhygar was the next to stir. He rolled restlessly on the pallet of grasses he'd collected to serve as his couch. Smiling to himself, Lone Wolf partially drew his sword from the scabbard which he'd been given back at Port Bax, and watched with amusement as Rhygar moved instinctively into a defensive half-crouch.

"Only me," Lone Wolf said.

"One of these days you'll find your gizzard on the opposite side of the ocean, if you carry on playing games like that," said Rhygar, his face only part-smiling. "But in the meantime I suppose I'll have to let you live—especially for the tale of the three Gourgaz."

"Every word of it true, sire," said Lone Wolf, nodding his head forward in mock-solemnity.

"Except perhaps for a few of them?"

"Quite true. Words are funny things, the way that they can make you say truths that happen to have not a grain of truth in them."

"I trust you told that to the three Gourgaz."

"Well, I would have, but they didn't give me time."

"That's the way with Gourgaz."

Rhygar shrugged histrionically as he climbed out of his sleeping blankets. Unceremoniously he kicked his three knights, one by one, and they grumpily greeted the new day. They rolled over—one of them yawning exaggeratedly—and stumbled off into the trees, searching for somewhere they could wash. A few minutes later they were cleanly groomed and ready to continue the journey.

The five of them had scrambled up on their horses when they saw ahead of them, higher up on the forest path, a group of six hooded riders. Lone Wolf felt for his sword. Rhygar and his knights seemed less concerned, though, and waved to the riders cheerfully.

"A fine morning, sirs!" cried Rhygar. "If you should be heading towards Hammerdal then, perhaps, we could ride together."

The hooded horsemen made no response, and once again Lone Wolf felt a shiver down his spine.

"I don't trust these people," he whispered to Rhygar. "There's something wrong about them."

"I don't trust 'em either," Rhygar replied softly, "but until we find out otherwise we've got to treat them as friends. And friends they may very well prove to be— who knows?"

In a louder tone Rhygar called out to the riders.

"Let us pass, I command you, for we are bearing a dispatch to our king, Alin."

Still the riders made no reply. The morning wind whipped through their cloaks, so that the cloth made a rhythmic slapping noise in the air. Behind them Lone Wolf could see the orange-blueness of the morning sky. Still, though, he could not see their faces. He had an icy premonition that these figures were no mortal riders.

"To stand in the path of a king's messenger is treason," Rhygar was bawling. "You can let us be, or you can become our travelling companions. Which do you choose?"

Still a silence from the hooded men.

"Do you mean us ill?" Rhygar was beginning to sound desperate. "Who are these, Lone Wolf?" he muttered.

"I think they may be Helghast."

"This far into Durenor? Surely they'd never dare!"

"I've slain a Helghast in my time," said Lone Wolf softly. "I wasn't lying when I told you about that over the campfire. They're difficult to kill—few mortal weapons can injure them. The spear I carry"—he lofted it—"will kill a Helghast, but I doubt that your swords would."

"My sword has slain creatures of every kind. Are you telling me that Helghast would be any different?"

"If these horsemen are Helghast, then, yes, I would tell you that."

Still there was the uncanny silence from above, nothing but the flapping of the dark riders' costumes in the breeze.

Rhygar turned away from Lone Wolf impatiently, and shouted once more at the waiting men.

"I have spoken to you reasonably," he yelled, his words half-fading into the trees all around them. "Now let me put it to you plain. Unless you speak to me, or turn to let us pass, our swords shall cut you limb from limb."

There was no reaction from the riders, except that one of their steeds whickered nervously.

"Then I must command my men to charge you," yelled Rhygar.

He spurred his horse up the narrow road, and his knights followed obediently behind him. They set up a great ululating shriek of battle, their swords swirling high in the air.

Lone Wolf screamed after them, but it was obvious that they could hear nothing above their own deafening racket.

"Wait!" he shouted. "In the name of Ishir, wait!"

His words had no effect on them. They were kicking their reluctant horses faster and faster into the gallop.

Lone Wolf's instincts were proved dramatically right when one of the hooded horsemen pulled from beneath his cape a black staff. It looked innocent enough, but Lone Wolf, trying to calm his terrified, pacing horse, recognized it instantly as a Darklord weapon. Once again he shouted a warning to Rhygar and the others, but once again they could hear nothing over the sound of their battle-cries.

The rider pointed his staff with elaborate care towards the feet of Rhygar's horse, and touched the shaft gently. A streak of blue flame shot out from the end of the staff; where it struck the ground beneath the envoy's horse there was a great eruption of earth. The animal reared up on its hind legs, screaming in a mixture of astonishment and pain, and threw Rhygar, turning and twisting through the air, into a deeply packed clump of bushes.

The knights hurtled their swords through the bodies of their foes, yelling mindlessly.

The swords had no effect.

Lone Wolf, still trying to calm his horse, cursed loudly, knowing that no one could hear. Whoever had tried to slay him during his long journey from Holmgard was trying to do so again. He believed it was the old man who could fly above the clouds, the man whom he now thought of as Vonotar.

These thoughts slid through his mind far more swiftly than time itself.

From his belt he drew the sword that Viveka had given to him. His friends were dying, and it was incumbent upon him to save their lives.

Agony shot through his mind.

One of the Helghast was trying to strike him dead in the same way that its fellow had in the copse near to the edge of the Durenor forest.

Raising his left arm as if to shield his head, Lone Wolf reached back with his right to grip the spear. As soon as his fingers curled around its shaft he felt a surge of blessed relief. As before, he knew that he was experiencing pain, but he didn't mind it any longer.

He felt a smile of cruelty cross his face, and then he gave vent to a vulpine howl.

He hammered his heels against the sides of his horse. It responded immediately and thundered up the hill. Lone Wolf could feel the blood-lust coming into his mind and he knew that, whatever happened, he would fight to the death. He was remotely aware that his voice was calling a high note, like an echo, magnified a millionfold, of the scream of the wind through the trees.

A Helghast was stooping from its horse to drive its black blade through the body of one of Rhygar's knights. Lone Wolf's spear pierced it through the chest, and it vanished with a thin wail. The knight, blood covering the face of his chain-mail helmet, shouted gratefully as he rolled over and over, dodging the churning feet of the horses, holding his arms up to protect himself from the ruthlessly pounding hooves. Lone Wolf backed his horse away, looking around for another enemy to attack, and then saw that three of the Helghast were charging towards him, their hoods now pulled back from their faces to reveal their rotting skull-like features. He held up his spear defensively, but they took no heed of it, their eyes piercing him like daggers as they galloped towards him. His horse, terrified, backed away still further . . . and suddenly Lone Wolf was tumbling through the air, falling downwards and seemingly forever downwards, as branches buffeted him from side to side. Then he felt a sickening jolt, as the hard earth slammed against his body.

He came to rest, stunned, in a tangle of bracken. His breath was coming with difficulty. He stared intently at a thin spread of bracken only an inch or so from his nose, and tried to concentrate on it—anything other than feel the agony of his windedness. From somewhere far above him he could hear the inhuman squawks of the Helghast as they savaged Rhygar's knights and the screams of those men as they died.

A hand grabbed his shoulder.

He shrugged it away, annoyed. Wasn't he just getting comfortable here in his bed of bracken?

The hand pulled more firmly, and Lone Wolf suddenly believed that this was a Helghast tugging at him, wanting to pull him upright so that it could kill him more slowly. He spat at the bracken, and turned himself over ponderously, bringing his sword uselessly up in front of him.

The bruised and bloodied face confronting him was that of Rhygar.

"Take the form of my friend, would you!" shouted Lone Wolf, still convinced that this was a Helghast.

"Shut up," Rhygar muttered. "We've got to get away from this place."

"But what about your men?"

"There's nothing we can do for them now."

An anguished screaming tormented the air above them. One of the knights was dying slowly.

"There's no more help we can give them," said Rhygar.

"We could kill more of the Helghast," Lone Wolf insisted, the redness of his killing frenzy returning to the front of his mind.

"Don't be a fool, Lone Wolf. We can best serve Sommerlund by escaping—*now*. Follow me, for the sake of Ishir!"

Still bemused, Lone Wolf allowed himself to be dragged further down the hill by Rhygar. They seemed to be making a tremendous amount of noise as they crashed through the low-lying branches which reached out to trip them, but Rhygar took little notice; the sounds they made were being drowned by the sadistic whoops of the Helghast on the ridge above them.

"From here on we move across country," said the older man roughly. "If there are Helghast here, then they must be infesting the rest of the land. No road is safe for us now."

"The Helghast . . . " Lone Wolf panted, his chest crying out for relief, " . . . I think they came for me alone!"

Rhygar paused momentarily, and looked at Lone Wolf with something akin to contempt.

"That's as may be," he said, "but it was the lives of my knights they took. These were good men—I valued them not just as comrades in arms but as friends. Remember their deaths as you journey to Hammerdal. If you fail to earn their lives I shall pursue you and make sure that your death is every bit as painful as theirs.

"Now let's stop all this talking and start getting away from here."

2

Banedon had been reading a book.

It wasn't a very good book, but centuries before some member of the Brotherhood of the Crystal Star had painstakingly transcribed it, adding luridly coloured marginal illuminations two or three times every page, and Banedon felt that he should respect this unknown person's endeavour by forcing himself to read on until the end. He turned the final page and put the book down beside his chair.

He looked at the silent form of Alyss, but as ever there was no change. He found himself irrationally furious with her. He had now lost count of the number of days and nights he had been incarcerated up here. At first tending her had been a labour of love, but now it had become a heavy burden, seeming to weigh down upon him with as much force as if it were a physical object. Would he never be allowed to escape from this room?

3

For several hours they ran without stopping for rest. Lone Wolf's limbs soon began to scream for mercy, but every time they did so he looked at the seemingly untiring figure of Rhygar and forced himself to keep up with the older man.

By late in the day they were in the foothills of the Hammerdal mountains. The air was fresh and pleasantly cool; on any other day it would have been a marvellous time to enjoy a gentle walk. As it was, the two of them were gasping for each fresh breath of air. Lone Wolf's clothes were once again almost as tattered and stained as they had been when he had arrived at the consulate. His weapons felt as if they were made of lead, dragging him down at every pace. He could only conjecture how Rhygar, still clad in his heavy chain-mail armour, must feel.

They were coming closer to what seemed to be the mouth of a colossal cave, a great inky maw in the mountainside. Lone Wolf looked at it with some dread—his experiences over the last couple of weeks with caves and tunnels had given him little reason ever to want to enter another, and he was certain that this was where Rhygar was leading him.

A little while later, Rhygar confirmed his worst fears. He slowed down in the shelter of a small granite outcrop and waved to Lone Wolf to stop. The two of them collapsed side by side for some minutes on the unyielding stone, listening to each other's harsh, exhausted breathing. They were overlooking a wide but deserted road, which cut easily through the landscape. A few birds could be seen as silhouettes drifting lazily across the sky, on their last forays before nesting down for the night. The sky was a hazy blue-grey when Rhygar sat up and pulled some food from his pack.

"Here," he said, passing Lone Wolf some bread and dried meat, "you'd better eat this."

"Not hungry," Lone Wolf breathed hoarsely. The air felt rough-edged in his throat; his chest seemed ready to explode.

"Then have some water"—Rhygar proffered a flask—"and after that eat some food. You'll need it. You've got a long way to go before you'll be able to rest again."

Lone Wolf took the flask and forced himself to drink sparingly. The pounding of the blood in his ears was beginning to become bearable at last; there was no longer a pinkish rim around everything he looked at.

"Where are we heading?" he said.

Rhygar jerked behind him with his head towards the vast hole in the mountainside.

"That's Tarnalin," he said. He took back the water flask and drank a little himself. "Thousands of years ago, during the Age of the Black Moon, people dug out this tunnel and two others like it through the Hammerdal mountains. It's your only way to reach the capital— unless you want to try your chances over the tops of the mountains themselves. Few people have tried that and succeeded. No, the tunnel's your only way."

Lone Wolf shivered. Now that it was getting darker, he could see that the entrance to Tarnalin was not as midnight-black as it had seemed earlier.

"You may be lucky," Rhygar was saying, "and find a merchant or some other traveller who will make room for you on his wagon. But I shouldn't think so. There's something very wrong here." He pointed forwards, spilling crumbs from his hand. "Normally, day or night, there's traffic on that road—people going to or from Hammerdal. As you can see, there's nothing now. The Darklords must have sent their Helghast into Durenor in force—that's the only explanation I can think of. Ishir alone can tell what it's like inside Tarnalin. We can only hope that the Helghast haven't slaughtered their way to the capital."

Lone Wolf felt his gorge rise. He had seen enough massacre. He had a revolted premonition of what the scene inside Tarnalin might be like.

"We've got to carry on," he said, conscious that his voice sounded reedily thin.

"No," said Rhygar.

"What do you mean?"

"I mean that from here you must carry on alone."

"But why?"

Lone Wolf found himself on the verge of tears. Surely the warrior couldn't be proposing to desert him now?

"As you were saying this morning, someone must have told the Darklords about you. It's you the Helghast are after. We can only pray that they don't realize quite how important you are. If I were commanding the Helghast"— Rhygar took a mouthful of the dried meat and chewed it ruminatively, scratching his chin with a grease-streaked hand—"I'd plan to stop you here, at the mouth of Tarnalin. They'll know that you have to go through one of the tunnels to reach Hammerdal. It's easier for them to lie in wait for you here than to comb the entire countryside."

"Then surely I need you beside me more than ever?"

"No, because once we were in the tunnel the two of us would be like rats in a trap." The soldier turned to look at Lone Wolf, and smiled. "But I'm trusting that they won't have the imagination to think that one of us might remain behind, out here."

Lone Wolf nodded glumly, abruptly looking away. It made sense. And, if only one of them could carry on into the tunnel, it was logical that it should be him, for no one else could retrieve the Sommerswerd from the palace of King Alin. But he didn't want to look Rhygar in the eyes right now, because he knew that what the soldier was proposing to do was to sell his own life dearly in order to delay the Helghast that would certainly try to follow Lone Wolf into Tarnalin.

"You're a very good friend indeed," he said softly.

"I thank you."

There was an awkward silence between them, and then Rhygar spoke again.

"But it's not just a friend to you that I am, young comrade, it's a friend to Sommerlund and Durenor as well. I've no wish to see the two realms that I love enslaved by those swine that Naar has vomited into Magnamund. If my life can spare Sommerlund and Durenor from that then I'll consider it well spent. Now come on: eat."

Lone Wolf ate, feeling guilty. Everywhere he went, people died. Some of them were good, some of them not so good, and some of them merely innocent. Now here was a valiant man set on going to an early grave so that Lone Wolf's life could be preserved. He knew that it wasn't exactly like that—that his life in itself was unimportant—but that was the way it *felt*. He didn't have the words to express any of this, but when he allowed himself to look back at Rhygar again he saw that the soldier's eyes, watching him, were sympathetic; Rhygar knew what he was thinking and understood it completely.

"Then I suppose," said Lone Wolf lightly, trying to keep all of his emotions out of his voice, "that it's about time I was moving along. You'd better take this." He passed Rhygar the spear he had captured, allowing himself for one last time to run his thumb along its mouldings. "You won't have a chance against the Helghast without it." *Or even with it*, he thought sadly, *but it'll help you to hold them back for a little longer, and that might be just long enough to make the difference between Sommerlund's damnation and its doom.*

"I thank you," said Rhygar. Again they were speaking formally.

Lone Wolf clapped the man softly on one armour-clad shoulder and began to make his way down towards the tunnel-mouth.

He couldn't bring himself to look back.

4

He moved cautiously to the edge of the tunnel entrance, trying to will himself to blend in with the darkened background of the hillside. Now that he was this close he could see that the interior of Tarnalin was in fact quite brightly lit: along each of its two side walls there was a line of torches, stretching away into infinity. While one part of him was relieved about this—it meant that he wouldn't be travelling in darkness—another part realized that it would make him incredibly vulnerable during the early few moments when he slipped into the tunnel: his dark shape would be dramatically backlit for anyone observing the tunnel-mouth from outside.

There was no right time to make his move—each was as bad as the next—and so he waited until his instincts prompted him to slip as unobtrusively as he could over Tarnalin's lip.

The tunnel was perhaps a hundred feet high and a hundred feet wide, and it echoed stilly at him as he clung to a side wall. It was obvious from the litter and detritus scattered about that it was usually heavily used, but now there was no living thing he could see. Just a few yards away, however, lay an overturned fruit cart. From the condition of the fruit that had been spilled across the road, it had not been there for long. Further away lay the corpse of a boy, his head almost severed from his body, his arms outstretched on the hard road-surface as if he were desperately clutching for something that was just beyond his reach.

Lone Wolf moved forward as quietly as possible, hugging the tunnel wall, trying to make his limbs move gently and smoothly, breathing slowly and fluently, forcing himself to act calmly. As he went further into Tarnalin he could see more evidence of destruction: horses, vehicles and humans were tossed into bizarre positions. Nothing was moving except the light from the torches. He sensed the mass of the mountain pressing down heavily from above as he skittered along the wall. A few days ago some of what he was now seeing would have sickened him, but the time for that was long past: now all he felt was a sort of dulled, throbbing loathing for whoever or whatever had perpetrated this carnage.

As he drew further away from the tunnel's mouth he began to believe that he had indeed been able to slip into it without being seen. He imagined Rhygar still maintaining his lonely vigil out on the hillside, and prayed that the man would be able to escape safely, come the morning. Now Lone Wolf felt more confident, and he moved away from the wall to follow his quickest possible path through the debris. He ran from each piece of cover to the next, always mindful that there could be a party of Helghast waiting to ambush him up ahead. He was starkly aware of his loneliness, seeing himself as a tiny speck of life moving across a flat plate, watched by a giant figure which could, at any time it chose, reach down to snuff out his life at the touch of a finger. Once he even caught himself looking upwards apprehensively, half expecting to see a huge hand descending inexorably towards him.

A flit of movement caught his eye, and immediately he went into a crouch, shielding himself behind the body of a carthorse which had died on its back, with its legs splayed crazily in the air. Lone Wolf leant against its cold body and for a moment thought that he could hear its heart still beating—then realized that the pulse he heard was his own.

But he could hear some other sound, too, as if a scrap of paper were being blown by a mild breeze across a deserted street.

Which was probably what it was.

Still, he moved with all the caution at his command as he raised his head to peer over his gruesome cover.

At first he could see nothing apart from more desolation, but then his eye was caught by motion about a hundred yards away, over towards the left-hand wall of the tunnel.

He stared in that direction, and as he did so he felt his eyes move into some new form of focus, so that he could see what was happening with an almost surreal clarity. He was so fascinated by this new-found ability that he almost forgot to take in what he was actually looking at.

On top of one of the crashed wagons was perched a ratlike creature—but far larger than any rat that Lone Wolf could ever have conceived. It was at least two feet long, not counting the tail, and it was eating an apple, which it held daintily in one of its forepaws.

At first he assumed that this was just some sort of large scavenging rodent which had bred down here in the tunnel, but then he noticed that the beast was something more than that. There was intelligence in its movements, as it looked warily about it in case of disturbance. And placed ready beside it was a spear hacked off halfway along the shaft, so that it would be the right size for the creature to use. Even more convincing than this was the fact that the rodent was wearing a patched leather jacket.

Hmm, thought Lone Wolf, watching the creature with amused absorption. *Intelligent enough to be able to use human artefacts but not actually to make them. I wonder if that creature's friendly? It's too small to do me much harm, anyway, so I might as well . . .*

He stood up quite openly, skirted the dead horse, and walked forwards, holding his hands out to each side, showing that they were empty of any weapons. He smiled ingratiatingly, at the same time realizing that there was no reason to believe that the creature could distinguish between a human smile and a contortion of hatred.

The beast saw him instantly and froze. Its beady black eyes were fixed on Lone Wolf as he continued to walk towards it. Its whiskered nose sniffed to and fro in the air.

Then the animal reached out a tentative paw for the spear by its side.

Lone Wolf, with his left hand, brushed the hilt of his sword, then moved the hand aside again. The gesture was just enough to convey his meaning: *I'm armed too*. The creature quite evidently received the message, because it withdrew its own paw, nodded with human-like solemnity, and then continued to watch his every move.

"Who are you?" said Lone Wolf, trying to keep any threatening note out of his voice.

But the sound startled the creature.

Throwing its half-eaten apple to one side, it grabbed its spear and was gone with a scuttle of claws over the back of the wagon.

Lone Wolf broke into a run.

"Hey!" he shouted. "I don't mean you any harm!"

He saw the end of its tail disappearing into a narrow side-tunnel.

He was tempted to let it go and carry on his way. But he'd been fascinated by the intelligence of the animal. He wanted to know more about what it was and where it came from. He swiftly rationalized his curiosity: for all he knew, this creature and its kind might be in league with the Helghast that had carried out the massacre in Tarnalin; if so, it would surely be going to report his presence to his enemies, and must be stopped at once.

Some instinct told him that the animal was far from hostile, but he pushed away the thought.

He chased into the narrow tunnel, and found himself having to duck and weave as he ran. To the rodents the passage must seem large, but it was barely wide enough to fit a human being. It seemed to have been designed by some crazy architect, because it twisted and turned unexpectedly. In the gloom Lone Wolf was constantly bruising his body against sharply angled corners and unseen protrusions.

After a short while he decided that further pursuit was pointless: much better to pick his way back to the main tunnel and make the best speed he could through the mountain. But then he saw a glow of light ahead of him, and decided to keep going for just a moment or two longer.

It was easier to see where he was going now, thanks to the steadily brightening light, and he moved carefully, dodging obstacles and holding his sword firmly against his side, trying to make as little noise as he could. For the last few yards he went on hands and knees.

The tunnel opened into a vast, vaulted cavern, lit by the flames of a thousand torches. The air was filled with industry, as things were dragged across the floor or thrown from one place to another, and there was a constant chorus of high-pitched squeaking. Hundreds upon hundreds of the rodents were crowded into the cavern, and in the torch-light they were zealously sorting through a great stack of oddments—clothing, food, weapons, small items of furniture, rugs and carpets, all the flotsam and jetsam of human culture. As Lone Wolf looked on, he saw one of them investigating a clock, looking at it upside down and from the rear, and then finally throwing it away with a resigned shrug as if to say that that particular object was worthlessly incomprehensible. Another was having similar difficulties with a book, but for the most part it was obvious to Lone Wolf that these creatures were treating the objects they were sorting with a fully intelligent knowledge of the function of each one.

The individual he had been following was squeaking excitedly at one of the largest of its fellows. This animal was well over three feet tall, and was dressed in an imposing brightly coloured cloak made of a patchwork of silks. It looked up towards him, and saw his face peering from the tunnel entrance.

It made a few swift gestures, reinforcing them with squeaked commands, and a number of the animals around it moved with swift efficiency to seize weapons. They were wielding daggers as if they were swords, but it was plain to Lone Wolf that they knew exactly how to use them—and the sharp blade of a dagger can kill just as finally as a sword.

He cursed his folly and his curiosity. He had little chance of escaping back the way he had come, for the passage was too narrow for him to make good speed—the nimbly moving creatures would catch him in no time. He slumped irritatedly down against the passage wall and wondered how he could convey to the animals that he meant them no harm.

Suddenly he remembered the little stone bottle that Kelman had given him. For some reason he'd kept it, always thinking that it had really been a useless gift but then relenting, remembering the circumstances under which he had received it. Now he could hear Kelman's dying words again—hear him saying that the bottle contained the Gift of Tongues. Of course, the bottles that Kelman had been so fond of also contained the Gift of Tongues—anything as strong as wanlo could make you talk until the day was done—but the irascible captain had been meaning something different.

Lone Wolf fumbled the bottle from his breast pocket and with difficulty pulled out its little nut-like stopper. Watching nervously as the armed rodents advanced determinedly towards him, he put the neck of the bottle to his lips and took a wary sip. The liquid tasted warm, yet it stung the inside of his mouth. He felt colours quickly spreading throughout his body, and then . . .

. . . and then it was as if he were a changed person. The world juddered into a different perspective, and he saw the animals as if they were human beings, just like himself. Furthermore, he understood exactly what they were saying: "Big, but not too big."—"Why should he die?"—"Some of the humans hate us! We can't let him go!"—"I'm thirsty."—"Gashgiss right when he tell us kill this human."

"Wait!" Lone Wolf shouted. His voice felt peculiar on his tongue. He realized that he was speaking in squeaks, but yet the words, when they echoed back to him from

the far sides of the chamber, sounded to him like Sommlending words. "I've got no wish to harm you!"

The effect was dramatic. All the rodents stopped whatever they were doing and stared at him blankly. Reassuringly, the armed detachment did the same. Lone Wolf
realized suddenly that these creatures had never before
heard a human being speak to them in their own language.

"Please don't attack me. Here. I'll show you how much
I trust you."

Lone Wolf tugged his sword from its sheath and tossed
it down on the floor. After a few moments' internal debate
he threw his dagger down as well. The stone bottle was
still in his fist, and he gripped it firmly, thinking that
if the worst came to the worst, and if these creatures
proved indeed to be allies of the Helghast, at least he'd
be able to brain a few before he died.

The tall creature in the silk cloak moved easily forwards, brushing aside the guards he had sent to attack
Lone Wolf. His paws were trembling and his whiskers
aquiver, but otherwise he betrayed no signs of nervous-
ness; he was like an experienced diplomat receiving an
envoy from a minor country.

"You are an intruder among us," he said sternly. "Kindly explain yourself."

Lone Wolf muttered a few words to the effect that he
was an innocent journeyer through Tarnalin, that he was
horrified by the scenes of massacre, that he had always
admired creatures with long whippy tails, that . . .

"You're not a Durenese man-man?" interrupted the tall
creature, gesturing away with his paw Lone Wolf's flow
of excess words.

These creatures were far more intelligent than he had
thought. He himself would have had difficulty in telling
a Durenese from a Sommlending with any degree of cer-
tainty, yet this imperious rodent had spotted the difference at once. Lone Wolf realized that he wasn't playing
about with lovable pets: this—man?—might not be his

intellectual equal, but he was at least as shrewd as many human beings would like to be. So Lone Wolf abandoned his patronizing tones and explained that yes, indeed, he was a Sommlending, and that he had been entrusted with an urgent mission. He deliberately avoided all details of his mission, and he could tell by the rodent's eyes that he understood precisely why Lone Wolf was keeping certain things from him.

"My name is Gashgiss," said the tall creature when Lone Wolf had finished, "and I welcome you, on behalf of all of us here, to our lair. You are the only man-man ever to have come to our lair and to be permitted to escape with his life. As long as you are not one of the blackscreamer-men?"

A little hiss of hatred sprang up among the animals, and Gashgiss silenced it with a firm wave of his paw.

Lone Wolf jumped to the conclusion that "black-screamer-men" were Helghast.

"If I were a Helghast, would I be speaking to you like this?"

"Could be."

The two of them stared at each other for a few moments.

Then Gashgiss laughed, showing two rows of brown teeth.

"No, you're not a blackscreamer-man. You're a man-man. Join us here among the Noodnic-men."

Still a little wary, Lone Wolf jumped down from his perch and picked up his sword and dagger, stowing them away with an easy confidence which he didn't quite feel. He noticed out of the corners of his eyes that many of the Noodnics felt similarly about him; the armed guards kept their weapons ostentatiously ready to hand. However, Gashgiss seemed to experience no such distrust, for he gave a merry smile and sheathed his own small sword, beckoning Lone Wolf to follow him.

In the very centre of the chamber there was a raised platform, and it was there that Gashgiss led Lone Wolf.

They talked for some while, sipping at drinks which tasted to Lone Wolf like sewer-water. The Noodnics, it seemed, infested all of the side-tunnels off Tarnalin. These had been built by the original architects, thousands of years earlier, as storage vaults and the like, but long ago the Durenese had forgotten about them. Nowadays they were inhabited only by the Noodnics, who survived by scavenging all the items of food and clothing that fell from the many carts and wagons that daily coursed through Tarnalin—indeed, some of the more superstitious drivers even made a point of throwing a small part of their cargoes to the road. In return for the living they made from the traffic, the Noodnics kept an alert patrol for hazards—in the way of floods or rockfalls—which might threaten the integrity of the tunnel, and warned the Durenese of these as soon as they could. The two species had a tacit agreement never to interfere with each other, and in general this worked out well. However, only that day, a party of different creatures—the "blackscreamer-men"—had come galloping into Tarnalin and had started to slaughter everything in their way, human and Noodnic alike. According to Gashgiss there had been only two Helghast, but Lone Wolf privately doubted the figure. The Noodnics had fought bravely alongside their human friends—Lone Wolf looked sceptical, but Gashgiss insisted—until even they had been driven back by force of arms: the "blackscreamer-men" were impervious to blades and arrows. Now the tunnel was deserted, and only the bravest or the most foolhardy—Gashgiss looked contemptuously at the individual who had led Lone Wolf here—ventured out into it.

A pair of male Noodnics approached them in stately fashion and offered them fruit. Lone Wolf accepted a Sommlending apple, Gashgiss a Cloeasian banana. Lone Wolf watched entranced as the rodent devoured the fruit, starting at one end and eating it skin and all. He was almost too diverted to eat his apple, although he was conscious that etiquette dictated that he should.

When Gashgiss had finished his banana he licked his lips in a satisfied manner and then patted them dry with his paws. He reached out to do the same for Lone Wolf, but Lone Wolf indicated that this would be in strict contravention of human custom, and Gashgiss eased himself away again.

"The blackscreamer-men are still in Tarnalin," he said, eyeing the claws of one paw with some interest.

"Are they indeed?" Automatically Lone Wolf reached for his spear, and then remembered that he had left it with Rhygar; once again he muttered a prayer that the warrior had escaped safely, but at the same time he cursed the fact that he no longer had the weapon. If he could have slain the waiting Helghast with it . . . but then perhaps there were too many of them for him to fight, even armed with the spear. He subsided, and listened to Gashgiss prattling on.

"I will ask some of my people to guide you past where the blackscreamer-men are waiting in ambush for any human who tries to pass through Tarnalin," the rodent offered.

"I can pay you," said Lone Wolf eagerly, feeling in his pockets, but Gashgiss raised a paw in protest.

"We Noodnics have other ways of being rewarded than by being given money," he said, a little stiffly. "To convince you of our honesty, I will escort you myself."

Lone Wolf sensed that this was a great honour, and acted accordingly. He offered to give Gashgiss his dagger, but the rodent haughtily refused. Then Lone Wolf promised that he would ask the authorities in Hammerdal to post notices proclaiming Gashgiss's heroism, and immediately he realized that he had said the right thing: the rodent leader seemed to swell to twice the size, and he pushed back his regal cap from his forehead, remarking with a good imitation of casualness that yes, that might be a suitable fee—especially if, perhaps, Lone Wolf could arrange for a portrait as well . . .

One of Gashgiss's servants provided Lone Wolf with

a cloth bag filled with fruit and buns, and then the two of them set off.

The tunnel through which Lone Wolf now found himself following Gashgiss was if anything even narrower and more convoluted than the one he had been in before. He frequently had to ask the Noodnic to slow down and wait for him as he negotiated some particularly awkward obstacle or bend. His progress was slowed down even further by the fact that the darkness was almost complete. Gashgiss seemed untroubled by this, and incapable of understanding why it should cause Lone Wolf any difficulties, but eventually he accepted it as one of humanity's minor inexplicable imperfections, and made allowances for it.

It must have been an hour or more later—an hour during which Lone Wolf felt that every possible part of his body had been bruised and battered—that a thin chink of light appeared and he realized gratefully that at last this torment was nearing its end. He walked straight into the back of Gashgiss, who had stopped suddenly. The Noodnic squeaked in pain as Lone Wolf stood on his tail.

When Gashgiss had recovered his composure, he took Lone Wolf's sleeve.

"Through there," he said. In the dimness Lone Wolf could just make out that he was pointing to the light ahead. "It's a crevice in Tarnalin's wall. Once you're through, turn left and you'll be heading for Hammerdal. The blackscreamer-men are behind us now."

The Noodnic jumped up on Lone Wolf's shoulder, scrabbling with his claws for stability.

"I leave you now," he said, and a moment later he had vanished into the darkness behind.

Lone Wolf shouted his thanks for the guidance and assistance, but all he heard in response were the echoes of his own voice.

A few minutes later he was squeezing himself with some difficulty through the narrow fissure, which brought him out into the main tunnel of Tarnalin, about three feet above the road. Moving as silently as he could, he dropped down into the roadway and stood looking around him warily. He was confronted by a further scene of mayhem and chaos, but again there was no sign of life, hostile or otherwise. It struck him grimly that he had no idea how far through Tarnalin he had progressed. Rhygar had told him that the tunnel was some forty miles in length but, for all he knew, he could have covered only a tenth of this. In the labyrinthine side-tunnels of the Noodnics it had been impossible to estimate distance.

He shrugged, every bone in his body aching. There was no sense in worrying about things over which he had no control. His plan was just to press ahead, making the best speed he could. He checked his equipment to make sure that nothing had been bent or damaged during his buffeting trip through the side-tunnels, and discovered to his horror that Gashgiss had been speaking the truth, but not the full truth, when he had said: "We Noodnics have other ways of being rewarded than by being given money." He had used the word "given." Apparently what he had meant was that the Noodnics preferred to be rewarded by *taking* money. All of Lone Wolf's gold had gone—presumably removed deftly from his clothing by Gashgiss during their journey through the darkness.

At first Lone Wolf was furious, and then he allowed himself a grin. Right now, money was the very last of his worries. The Noodnics were welcome to it for having saved him from the Helghast ambush.

He began moving very quickly indeed, flitting quietly from one piece of cover to the next, frequently checking behind him in case the Helghast might decide to check further along Tarnalin. The devastation here seemed less than it had been earlier, and he began to notice that, scattered among the corpses of the peasants and traders, there were the bodies of soldiers dressed in the red uniforms of the Durenese army. *So someone at last began to put up a resistance*, he thought ruefully. *It's just a pity they didn't get here any earlier. They could have saved thousands of lives if they'd been able to confront the Helghast before they entered the tunnel.*

Now more and more soldiers were among the dead. He could hear the echoing sound of many voices from the tunnel ahead, and he moved with greater caution than before. Perhaps the massacre was still in progress. His urge was to run towards it as fast as he could, to help whoever was fighting against Zagarna's vile spawn, but he immediately recognized that this would have been folly: it was far more important for him to reach Hammerdal, retrieve the Sommerswerd and, hopefully, to help bring the war to an end than to fight and possibly die in some minor skirmish.

He needn't have worried. Drawn up across the tunnel he saw a line of wagons and carts, forming a rudimentary barricade. Behind it was a large crowd of people, some shouting, some sobbing hysterically at the horror that had so recently occurred, others merely adding to the general hubbub. As Lone Wolf advanced the noise slowly trailed away, and he felt himself to be the object of a thousand eyes. He could almost hear the crowd collectively thinking: *How could he have survived? Surely he can only be another Helghast, sent to slaughter us all?*

Lone Wolf raised his hands in peace.

A tall knight, his shield embossed with the royal arms of Durenor, barked a few orders and then led a squad of about ten foot-soldiers towards him. All had swords drawn; clearly they were taking as few chances as possible. Lone Wolf smiled, but realized that a Helghast could smile, too. Two of the men looked utterly terrified when they were detailed to approach him more closely; he admired their discipline and courage as they nevertheless moved firmly to obey the order.

"Who are you?" snapped the officer.

"My name is Lone Wolf. I'm a Sommlending. I've been sent on an urgent mission to King Alin."

"How can we tell that you are speaking the truth? No human could have lived through what went on . . . back there." The officer jerked his head towards the tunnel behind Lone Wolf.

"It'll take me a while to explain—"

"You're too right it will."

Lone Wolf, moving slowly and deliberately so as not to startle the two soldiers nearing him, drew his sword and offered it to them, hilt-first. One of them took it, cautiously, and then with a little more confidence accepted Lone Wolf's dagger.

"Your backpack as well!" snapped the officer.

Lone Wolf obeyed. He felt uncomfortably naked. The two soldiers retreated, carrying his equipment, their swords still drawn and their eyes still fixed on him.

The officer moved smartly towards Lone Wolf, raising his visor. He had a prominent hooked nose, bushy sand-coloured eyebrows, and hard green eyes.

"Now, Sommlending, tell me why you're here—and don't make a false move, or my men will slay you. One more body among all these won't make much difference."

Lone Wolf explained as much of his mission as he felt was wise. He also told how the Noodnics had guided him past the place where the Helghast were lying in wait, but was deliberately vague as to the details: he had no wish to reward his little friends by encouraging the Durenese, at some future date, to clear the side-tunnels of what they would undoubtedly regard as vermin. The officer looked interested but unconvinced until Lone Wolf showed him the seal.

Instantly the man's demeanour changed.

"This is a friend," he said curtly to his soldiers. "Return his belongings to him immediately. Look sharp about it, you there! We must get moving. Quick, quick, man!"

Within moments the tall knight was leading Lone Wolf through the barricade of wagons, shouting at members of the crowd, who were gathering with eager curiosity around them, to make way. The sea of human forms parted reluctantly, so that it was as if Lone Wolf were looking down a long corridor of many-coloured clothing and faces. At its end he could see that several carriages, some military, others civilian, had been drawn up. The officer guided him towards one of these, and the two of them climbed into its musty-smelling comfort. One of the soldiers rapidly clambered up to take the reins.

"Hammerdal," the officer said crisply. "We must get back to Hammerdal without delay."

A crack of the whip, and Lone Wolf's head was thrown back against the panelling as the high-spirited horses erupted into movement.

4

THE SWORD OF
THE SUN

1

The swift-moving carriage rattled and jolted as it sped along the last few miles of Tarnalin. The way was clear now, and the horses were moving at a full gallop. The staccato pounding of their hooves and the rattle of the carriage's thin wheels on the hard road echoed back from the great tunnel's walls. The wooden frame of the carriage creaked and moaned. Lone Wolf and the officer had to half-shout to make their voices heard above the din.

The officer introduced himself as Lord Axim of Ryme, and Lone Wolf was impressed; this was one of the most important men in Durenor. Lord Axim was commander of King Alin's personal bodyguard. He had apparently been travelling with a large detachment of his men from Hammerdal to Port Bax when they had been confronted in Tarnalin by the Helghast—only he and a few of his soldiers had survived. Axim's hands shook as he described some of the worst of the Helghast's atrocities. Helped by many other travellers they had finally succeeded in erecting the rough barricade of wagons as a last desperate measure. Here Axim's voice faltered.

"But it's a funny thing, you know. I don't see how the barrier could have stopped them. They just seemed to give up. I don't know . . . "

Lone Wolf did know what had happened—or, at least, he was fairly certain—but he decided against telling Axim. Somehow the Helghast had been informed that he, Lone Wolf, was entering Tarnalin. The carnage they had carried out had simply been a way of passing the time until they had received that information. As soon as they'd known that their main prey was approaching, they'd given up slaughtering the Durenese and turned their attentions instead to the main task—killing Lone Wolf. But who could it have been who had told them? Who was it who had been able to track him all the way from Holmgard—who even now might be relaying back to Zagarna the fact that he was riding in a military coach to Hammerdal? The only clue he had was the name "Vonotar"—but who or what Vonotar could be was a mystery to him. He had heard of the magical powers of names and, although he distrusted and disliked magic in all its forms, he feared its powers, too. Perhaps Vonotar was a system of magic which the Darklord's minions were using to pinpoint his every move? He recalled uneasily his feeling, when he had been coming through Tarnalin, that he was like a tiny smudge of life being watched by a giant eye.

"Have you ever heard of Vonotar?" he asked Axim.

"No, never," the aristocratic officer replied tersely. "What is it? Why do you ask?"

Lone Wolf couldn't explain. If he said that someone or something called Vonotar was pursuing him, was trying to kill him at every stage of his journey, Lord Axim would assume that he was mad. That would make him begin, all over again, to doubt Lone Wolf's story. No, the question would have to remain unanswered.

He waved his hands vaguely, deflecting Axim's enquiry.

"Just a name I heard along the way," he said. "I don't think it's important."

But it *was* important; he knew deep inside himself that it was, and he resolved to keep asking people until he was given an answer.

The conversation turned to more banal matters, and Lone Wolf ate some of the food the Noodnics had given him. Axim offered him a flask, and Lone Wolf washed down the fruit and dried buns with sweet Hammerdal mead—too sweet, indeed, for his palate, but he was grateful for the liquid.

"It'll take us some hours to reach Hammerdal," said Lord Axim after a long pause. "You might be best to get yourself some rest."

Lone Wolf agreed. The mead had made him drowsy. He punched his backpack into a corner of the coach as a pillow and lay across the full length of the seat. He looked upwards, at the endless stream of torches moving past the carriage window, and their rapid succession of lights acted upon him hypnotically, so that he was counting their rhythmic passage as his eyes slowly closed.

For a while the flickering lights continued in his dream, but then they became the torches held aloft by the vast crowds of a victory parade. The masses of people gathered there were shouting his name. He was riding on a white horse—Janos, his old friend, given to him by Prince Pelathar—and accepting the praises of the crowd with humility. He knew that he had brought the Sommerswerd back from Durenor to Holmgard and had slain the Darklord Zagarna. The vast hordes of the Darklands had been scattered to the winds, and Sommerlund and all of the Lastlands had been saved. Of course he knew that the salvation could not last forever, that Naar would send some new threat to menace the Lastlands; but at the same time he was aware that he would be forever remembered in the legends of the Lastlands. And, however much he told himself that he had just been lucky, that it wasn't him in particular that the fates had selected to play this role in the history of his people, the feeling was good. He remembered Storm Hawk, and the way that his old tutor had frequently despaired over Lone Wolf's prowess—or lack of it—in his studies of the Kai Disciplines, and he wished with all his heart that his mentor could see him now. *Thank you, Storm Hawk,* he thought fervently, *for what you were able to make me.*

He was in daylight when he awoke, and for some minutes he stretched lazily on the comfortably upholstered seat, basking in the glowing pleasure of victory, feeling the adulation of all the coming generations lapping against him . . . and then he remembered abruptly that all of this had yet to happen, that indeed it might *never* happen.

He sat up crossly, rubbing his knuckles in his eyes to get rid of both the sleepiness and the dream itself, and stared out dourly over the countryside surrounding Hammerdal. The carriage was now bumping over a cobbled road. Opposite him, Axim had removed his helmet and was snoring regularly, his hooked nose trembling with each grating breath.

Lone Wolf's feelings of frustration didn't last long. A few miles ahead of them he could see the city of Hammerdal spread out generously across an evenly rolling plain. Unlike the other cities of the Lastlands this one had no fortified perimeter wall; the encircling ring of the Hammerdal mountains provided more protection than ever humans could create. Despite the distance, Lone Wolf could tell that it dwarfed even Holmgard in size and splendour. He was struck first by the profusion of flags and banners: they seemed to wave from every rooftop, from the tallest of the silvery gleaming towers to the squatter commercial buildings and even the commoner dwelling-places. The massed banners made the whole scene seem to ripple with blue and white—the colours of Durenor—and Lone Wolf had a momentary sensation that he was looking not at a city but at the surface of a multi-coloured sea.

As the carriage sped closer he could make out individual details. Dominating the whole city, crowning Hammerdal's only hill of any size, was the King's Tower, a vast edifice made of glass and stone. In the morning sunshine it presented a constantly changing pattern of liquid reflected light. Beneath it the city draped away, looking rather as if someone had thrown down a cloth of velvet, allowing it to fold as it would. Unlike many other cities, there were no poor areas of Hammerdal: the security of the surrounding mountains had given the city prosperity over the centuries, so that even its humblest citizen owned a pair of horses and a carriage to harness them to. The schools and colleges of the city were renowned all over the Lastlands, as were the riches of some of the merchants and bankers. Lone Wolf had heard that Hammerdal boasted also a magnificent museum, to which were brought the finest artworks and most mysterious relics from Durenor and the surrounding countries. He resolved that one day, in more peaceful times, he would return to this place and spend some weeks or months exploring its wonders.

Lord Axim awoke just in time to speak with a platoon of soldiers who were standing by the roadside. Clearly news had already reached here of the massacre in Tarnalin, and the army was taking what precautions it could. The carriage was waved on, and soon it was rattling over the paved streets of the city.

"To the King's Tower," Axim called up to the driver, and the man knocked on the roof to show that he had heard. He began to shout imperiously to people on the street to clear the way.

Lone Wolf regretted that they were moving quite so quickly. Through the windows he could make out just enough of the splendours of Hammerdal to know how much he wished to be able to examine them more closely. The streets were broad, with wide pavements on each side. People from a dozen countries or none thronged these walkways, the diversity of their rich costumes, many brightly coloured and textured with gleaming swathes of precious metals, presenting a shimmering tableau of magnificence. Children darted among the adults, shouting in their games, and here and there a space was cleared for the performance of a juggler, a fire-eater or an acrobat. Lone Wolf saw many broad shop-fronts in which were displayed elaborate dresses, exotic foodstuffs or exquisitely wrought jewellery.

Soon, though, they were out of the city's commercial area and were pressing on through streets surrounded by the tall, dignified dwellings of the nobility. Each was fronted by a well tended garden, and Lone Wolf saw many unfamiliar shrubs and small trees, some of them with leaves in unnatural-seeming colours—crimson, grey-blue, a startling cyan. There were few people on the pavements here, mainly mothers walking with their small children, or servants scurrying about on errands. From time to time they would be passed by mounted knights, with some of whom their driver exchanged a greeting.

Lone Wolf felt a building excitement inside him. In a time so short that it could be counted in minutes he would be ushered into the presence of King Alin; and not long after that, he felt confident, he would at last lay eyes on the Sommerswerd, the almost legendary weapon with which, over twelve hundred years ago, the first King Ulnar of Sommerlund had slain the Darklord Vashna at the battle of the Maakengorge. He didn't know whether to feel awe or elation—awe that he would be in the presence of this great weapon, or elation that he, alone among generations of the Kai, should have been selected to play this role. He grinned nervously at Axim, who returned his gaze stonily.

"This is hardly a time for smiling," said the knight.

"I'm sorry." Lone Wolf's face collapsed in embarrassment. He seemed to have violated some minor Durenese

104

ethic; he must remember to be wary of such things. "I just . . . I don't know what I was trying to say."

"When you reclaim the Sommerswerd, at the same time you drag all of Durenor into your war. Is that a cause for celebration? Perhaps for you it is. But for us Durenese, it is a sad day. I can remember fighting under Rhygar against the Ice Barbarians, and I saw things then that made the slaughter in Tarnalin seem like a child's idle game."

And it was *just an idle game—for the Helghast*, thought Lone Wolf, but he kept his peace. He remembered the sentinel at the edge of the Durenor forest expressing similar opinions. He imagined the way that he would feel if, as a Durenese, he were to find himself press-ganged into some remote war—although of course he knew, just as Axim must now be aware, that it wasn't a war that could remain remote forever. If Sommerlund fell to Zagarna's host, Durenor could not be far behind.

"Already there are Helghast in your country," he said softly, anxious not to offend the knight in any way. "Do you imagine that Zagarna cannot already be thinking about the conquest of Durenor?"

"No." Axim sighed, and stared distractedly out of the carriage windows as the elegant grey buildings marched by. "No, of course it has to be that our nation joins yours to fight off our mutual foe, and of course in the long run it would go all the worse for us if we didn't come to your aid now, but that doesn't mean that we have to enjoy the prospect of war. I've done enough killing in my life— I've no desire to do any more."

The knight leaned forward and looked at his armoured hand. He moved the fingers stiffly.

"But the ones you'll be killing—they're only the spawn of Helgedad!" said Lone Wolf.

"True, true. And the more that I kill of them the less of our country's children will die of their cruelty. But we Durenese believe that *all* life, however vile it may be, has a sanctity of its own. We would rather that these things did not have to happen."

Lone Wolf warmed to the man. He reached out and patted him on the knee. He, too, had often felt remorse after slaying Giaks, even though he knew that it was something that had to be done, and that the force animating the vicious spawn was not anything that could really be described as "life."

The gesture was enough for Axim; he knew what Lone Wolf was trying to convey, and he acknowledged it with a respectful nod. "So long as you don't just view war as an exciting game," he said sombrely. "That's all I need to know. It's a disgusting business, and if we could ever rid our world of the forces of Evil then it might never blight our lives again. It is our duty—indeed, our privilege—to be the ones to combat the Evil of Naar. But . . . well, as I said, we don't have to *like* it."

They relapsed into silence, further words unnecessary. The two of them were in complete understanding.

2

Alone in his gilded tower King Alin sat on a throne of carved ebony. His thoughts played like music across his mind—a funereal dirge, its pace solemn and slow, sometimes moving naturally into discordancy. He had known for weeks that this day would come, and he dreaded it.

He moved on the throne, so that he could see a different aspect of Hammerdal through one of the tower's countless tinted, prismatic windows. The boy would come—the boy who had been sent by Ulnar, but beyond that by the Sun God himself—and he would be bearing the Seal of Hammerdal. The king felt the forces of Darkness encroaching all around him. He had hoped that his reign would be recalled as one of peace and fulfillment for all the people under his sway, but he knew that now this could never be so. The youth would claim the Sommerswerd, as was the right of the Sommlending, and Durenor would be plunged into war. There would be slaughter in its rich fields and grasslands, and too many thousands of his people would die in agony, their last thoughts being not of the wisdom of their king but of the doom that the ages-old pact of Durenor with Sommerlund had brought to them.

He shifted his position again, and one of the sharp peaks of the Hammerdal mountains came into view. He looked at it with a sense of deep sorrow. It was sharp, like the point of a sword, and similarly it had no mercy for the lives it might destroy. The youth who was coming to claim the Sommerswerd would be like that, he was certain; a highly trained Kai killing machine who would rejoice in the blood-smell of battle. King Alin was not ashamed when he felt a tear trickle down his cheek. At the same time he knew that no mortal, however exalted, could change the pattern of the game that the Gods played: the course of future events was not something that he could hope to control—or that he should even have the temerity to seek to. Still . . . still . . . he wished that the Gods could have seen it within themselves to have hesitated for a few more decades until he had gone to some other world.

Alin looked resentfully at a marble dais in the centre of his throne-room. In the centre of its top there was an intricately wrought lock, made of gold. In the pocket of his white robe he bore, as he always did, as his fathers had done before him, the key to that lock. None of them had had to use the key: he would be the first of all his line.

He rested his hand on the arm of his throne and looked at it as if it were an alien creature, something which had nothing at all to do with him. He saw the wrinkles of its knuckles as if they were landscapes of a faraway country. The back of the hand was marked with liverspots, and he saw them as slowly growing cancers, intent upon invading his country. He had always felt that he and Durenor were in some way inextricable—just two very different manifestations of the same life-principle. In his mind he confirmed this notion as he looked at his blemished hand.

King Alin heard the sounds of marching feet on the stairway outside his throne-room and he returned to reality. As he had known for these long weeks, the noises heralded the arrival of one of his lords—he had been unable to decide which—accompanied by the Kai youth. Why the Kai should send someone so callow on this quest he had no idea; perhaps they felt that a boy would be less likely to be observed by the forces of Darkness, or maybe they had sent a hundred messengers, knowing that many of them would be murdered by agents of Zagarna as they made their way to Hammerdal, and this boy was merely the first to arrive. Alin didn't know, and the grief of what he perceived as his failure had wearied him so much that he didn't care. The time was at hand—the time that all the prophecies had predicted—when the Sommerswerd would be reclaimed and all of Durenor would be plunged into the miseries of war.

Alin called "Enter!" even before his sentries had knocked on the golden door of his throne-room.

He looked up sadly as he saw Lord Axim throw open the door and march in, followed by a youth whose cloak, though tattered and stained, was obviously that of a Kai. The boy looked apprehensive, and yet at the same time eager and expectant. With a wistful sweep of his gaze, Alin took in his sharp features and the tight, controlled way in which he moved.

A guard at the door called formerly: "The Lord Axim of Ryme and a Sommlending called Lone Wolf!"

Alin pushed the shout away with his hand. He knew tiredly who the pair of them were. *Poor Axim*, he thought, *one of the bravest and the best of all my subjects. He little deserves to be remembered in our histories as the man who led war to our shores.*

"I see you, Axim," said the king aloud. He rose from his throne and walked forward to greet his old friend. He saw the familiar hooked nose—like the beak of a bird of prey—and he almost found it within himself to smile as he recalled, as always, the way that at school they had all teased the studious boy about it. Alin and Axim embraced briefly and then the two of them stood back, hands on each other's shoulders, and looked each other in the face.

"I know," said the king. "Old friend, there isn't any need to tell me."

"The boy," said Lord Axim. "He's the last of all the Kai. He's come to us to claim the—"

"I told you, I know why he's come here. I've felt it all through myself for these last weeks. The terrible day when the Sommlending must retrieve the Sommerswerd is upon us. That the Kai have been destroyed—no, I did not know that, but I'm hardly surprised: Ulnar wouldn't have called upon us for the Sommerswerd if the crisis hadn't indeed been grave."

Lord Axim nodded sadly. His old friend had always had the gift of knowing something of the dark events that the future was going to bring.

Lone Wolf watched as the king beckoned Axim over to a couch on the far side of the room. Now that he was here he was finding the whole experience something of an anticlimax. Somehow he'd been expecting to be ushered in with a fanfare of trumpets, welcomed by a resplendent court, hundreds of nobles surrounding him on every side. Instead he saw two weary-looking men retreating quietly from him to start talking in softly susurrating tones, so that he could make out nothing of what they were saying. After a few minutes Axim returned to him and, with a few murmured words, removed the Seal of Hammerdal from his finger to show it to King Alin. The two men nodded sorrowfully over it, and then Lone Wolf saw them both turn to look fixedly for a moment at a block of what seemed to be solid marble, set centrally in the throne-room. Now they returned to their infuriatingly quiet stream of conversation.

Lone Wolf looked around him. The short sleep he had had on his journey from Tarnalin had refreshed him only partially. His excited anticipation had revived his energies, but now that he was merely being expected to stand and wait he was suddenly exhausted all over again. He moved his mind to cure some of the worst of his bruises, and then stood for a little longer, his feet apart on the flecked grey marble of the floor.

Finally he gave up. There were some soft-looking chairs on either side of the door and, ignoring all thought of courtesy, he moved over to throw himself down on one of them. Axim glared at him briefly, he was aware, but he consciously paid no attention to the look.

Lone Wolf was fascinated by the throne-room's windows. He moved his head from side to side and up and down, catching different facets of light and with them different facets of *life* as well. Here he could see, bathed in light green, two children playing with a hoop in a park, watched benevolently by an elderly servant; the detail was so sharp that he could make out the pale shine of their teeth as they laughed and shouted. Over there, through a different pane, he could see a merchant sitting in an upstairs room, moving piles of gold coins around on a mahogany desk, ticking off items on a list and sucking in his lips thoughtfully; the picture was tinted in a curious reddish-orange colour. Another window and another scene. Through an aura of silver mist he could see two young lovers speaking earnestly to each other, their faces locked into a trusting solemnity. Lone Wolf rapidly shifted his gaze, feeling a twinge of guilt, as if he were eavesdropping on their personal lives.

Alin coughed, politely, and Lone Wolf's attention returned to the throne-room.

The king had advanced to stand beside the marble dais in the centre of the chamber. Behind him, on the couch, Axim sat watching, his face drawn.

Lone Wolf stood, his head slightly bowed in a formality of respect.

Alin's voice was dusty, like an unused corridor in an ancient palace.

"I have little that I can say to you, Lone Wolf.

The time foretold so many generations ago has finally come. The Darklords have woken once more, and Sommerlund is on its knees. Durenor will arm herself to come to your aid, and the people of my country will gladly lay down their lives to turn back the forces of Evil."

He coughed again, moving his hands as if slightly embarrassed by the weight of his words.

"But more than that, you seek the sword—and of course it must be yours. I wish that this day had never dawned, and yet I give the sword to you gladly. Take it, with my blessings."

The tendons on his wrist stood out as he tried to control the trembling of his thin hand, the hand that held the key. He reached forwards, and with difficulty placed it in the lock.

Abruptly, as if trying to get the moment over with as quickly as possible, he turned the key.

The room was filled with a gentle humming. Alin took an involuntary step backwards.

The marble cover of the dais rose into the air and then slid sideways. It hovered over the stone floor for a moment, and then crashed down, shattering into myriad shards.

Lone Wolf was drawn forwards, slowly, one foot reluctantly following the other.

He came to the great stone coffin and looked down into it.

There, couched beside its jewel-studded scabbard on a bed of maroon velvet, glowing and pulsing with its own life, lay the great Sommerswerd.

The Sword of the Sun.

3

No one spoke for a minute or two, and then Alin said, almost shyly: "Wait, young Kai Lord, wait. If you are a true son of Sommerlund, then the sword will bequeath to you all of the powers bestowed on it by the wisdom of those who were here before us. If you are not . . ."

He let the words hang. Again he made that curious, half-embarrassed gesture with his hands.

He began to speak in words that were obviously a ritual, his eyes glassing over as his mind was filled by a timeless spirit:

When the Lastlands of Magnamund were only children,
There dwelt here a race that talked with the Gods.
The sun shone from their eyes, and the mountains
    trembled at their gaze.
The winds of the sky were their brethren, and the seas
    ebbed and flowed at their bidding.
They saw all of the past and all of the future,
And they saw that the day would come when they
    themselves would be only wisps of memory,
And that then there would be on the Lastlands your race
    and mine and the creatures of the Darkness.

And they spoke among themselves and with the Gods,
And the Gods said to them: "These things shall be."

Then the nameless ones saw also a golden strand running
    through all of time,
And they named this strand the Sommerswerd
And plucked it from time's fabric.
In their forge that rode upon the clouds
They wreathed the gold that came from time
And fashioned from it in the fires of their own minds
This sword.

Into the sword they placed their soul-stuff, singing as
    they gave themselves to it.
And they strewed their soul-stuff also among the
    mountains and the seas,
The forests and the rivers and the skies,

Leaving it there for the time when men and women
would come among the Lastlands.

This soul-stuff was their breath, and all may breathe it.
This soul-stuff was their blood, and all may drink it.
This soul-stuff was their dreaming, so that all may
dream their dreams.
But some who breathe, breathe only air,
And some who drink, drink only water,
And some who dream, dream only of night.

Yet those born of the spirit of Kai breathe of the nameless
ones, and drink their blood and dream their dreams,
And within them is the soul-stuff of the nameless ones
And of the sword.
They are one with the sword.
They are the sword, and the sword is them.

If you who stand before me are truly of the sword then
take it,
For at its touch you will be reunited with the nameless
ones
And the power of their thoughts shall be yours.
But if you are not truly of the sword, then go from this
place
And walk among the world, seeking for the faces of those
who dream the old ones' dreams,
And bring such a person here, for the soul-stuff of the
sword will marry with none other,
But rather bleed away into the eternity of night.

Take this sword, if you are its brother or its sister,
Take it, and be blessed by us who have gone before you.

The light of the sword filled the room—a blazing white-
ness that seared the eyes. Alin ceased his rhythmic chant,
and caught himself as he almost fell. Axim took a few
urgent steps towards his king, and then stopped, his eyes

113

narrowed against the sword's brilliance.

Alin looked at Lone Wolf, and the young Kai Lord—for he knew that now he was indeed a Kai Lord—saw that the king's own spirit had returned to him.

"Touch it," whispered Alin, his voice as dry as a desert breeze. "Touch the sword."

Lone Wolf watched his own right hand reach out, tentatively at first and then with more purpose. It moved of its own accord, without his control, to touch the hilt of the Sommerswerd.

There was a flash of light so piercing that it seemed to devour all of reality, to sound like a thunderclap, to be in itself all that there was of Aon captured in a single moment.

And Lone Wolf felt the sword's hilt, and it was warm and almost soft to his touch, welcoming him.

A feeling of miraculous ecstasy flooded through him. He saw himself as the focus of a million minds, a place where the past and the future came together. Now his mind acted in concert as he raised the sword high above his head, and a terrible wordless shout came from his lips. He cried in an infinity of voices, as all the spirits of the dead and the as yet unborn spoke through him in a single moment. He was there and yet he was not there. He heard the scream of all of the words of Aon, and

colours, a wash of colours mingling and twisting together, seemingly tied together into smoky ropes as they weaved and whirled all together, filling his vision until there was nothing else but colour, and the colours spun themselves together until they were the clearness of the air . . .

sounds that clashed together, mixing and mingling until they became the bitter-sharp taste of the petals of yellow roses, sounds that were blindly seeking towards the skies . . .

a pain that in its exquisite sharpness was a hard metallic light, conquering all of his body, scented with the overpow-

114

ering odour of rosemary, arcing his body until he felt as if his body were a bow, the cells of the wood straining away from each other, and the tiny fragment of himself that remained feeling the searching probes of merciless knives . . .

He was in a place where time was a young woman steadfastly playing on a xylophone made out of the years. She looked up at him and smiled, then returned to the embrace of the music. She bit her lower lip as she concentrated, her hands moving too swiftly to be seen as the hammers touched the bones of the instrument. He watched her face as she played, seeing the greenness of her eyes and the arch of her thin, red eyebrows above. At one moment she was a stately courtier, and the visible music that sprang from her hands was an elegant dance; at the next she was a gamine, clothed in ragged garments of the colours of an autumn forest. She looked up at him again, her forehead this time ruffled. And then she threw the hammers away into a distant darkness, reached her hands high above her head, her small breasts pushing against the matted felt of her tunic as she twined her fingers and became the entirety of . . .

4

. . . reality.

He was standing in the throne-room, the lights of the tinted windows spreading like stains across the floor. The sword was now by his side, its tip touching cold stone. He felt exhausted, yet at the same time filled with a surging of spirit; his whole body was trembling with energy that was seeking some form of release.

Alin was clutching the side of the empty marble coffer.

"The sword is yours," the king said, his voice almost weeping.

"And I am the sword's," said Lone Wolf.

5

THE BATTLE OF THE DEAD

1

The days sped by, and Lone Wolf began to keep a count of them. He was living in King Alin's Tower, and all of his comforts were provided for; he was all too well aware of the fact that, after his weeks of adversity, all that he really wanted to do was to relax into the luxury of soft beds and fine foods, but at the same time the new consciousness which he felt now that he had been united—or, so it seemed to him, reunited—with the Sommerswerd was telling him that during each of the days that he spent in idleness Sommlending were dying in their hundreds or their thousands. He knew that there was nothing that he could do to stop this, and yet he felt guilt weighing down upon him, colouring every smallest thing that he did. *Here am I, raising this cup of wine to my lips, and yet how many are screaming their last, hundreds of miles away in Sommerlund, as I do this? Now I walk along one of Hammerdal's wide streets, people falling back from me because they know who I am and why I am here,*

*and yet in the same vision that I see the riches of their garb
and listen to the music of their accents, I see also a woman
spitted on a Giak sword and hear a man's cry as his children
are slaughtered before him. And here I sit at a laden table,
eating fruits of many colours, listening as the king tells me
the tales of his ancestors, but intermingled among his words
are those which will no longer be spoken . . .*

There was no escape from it.

He flirted with the maidens of the court, played games
of samor with them and with their brothers, joked with
the older men and women or talked earnestly of the fate
of Sommerlund, but all the time he knew that he was
just acting out a role. He had never been designed to be
a charmingly mannered member of an elegantly attired
court. The sword which he carried always at his belt told
him that he should now be fighting to defend his country
from the armies of Evil, yet at the same time it reassured
him that he could best serve his countryfolk by waiting
here, in Hammerdal, until the Durenese army had been
mustered and the war-fleet of this great nation was ready
to put to sea.

It was a warm afternoon, and he was sitting in one of
Alin's many stately gardens. The smell of the crushed
herbs of the lawn was in his nostrils, the sound of exotic
birdsong in his ears. He smiled at a young girl—King
Alin's daughter, no less—her face painted in the pale-
ness that was fashionable in the court, her hair superbly
coiffed, her dress tailored to emphasize decorously the
contours of her body—and all he could see was Qinefer,
dressed in coarsely woven clothes of poorly dyed wool,
her crinkling black hair in disarray, a trickle of sweat
running down the side of her nose.

This was the wrong place for him. His soul screamed
it to him, and yet there was nothing he could do to take
himself away. He had to act the part of a visiting courtier,
to move graciously in the slowly spinning gavotte that was
courtly life. At least for now.

Each evening, he and Axim, together with the king,

met in the throne-room to discuss how Durenor's preparations for war were proceeding, and to make hazy plans about how they could best save Holmgard and Sommerlund. Lone Wolf tried to inject urgency into these discussions, telling the two older men that he, alone except for the Sommerswerd, could set sail for Sommerlund and slay Zagarna. Always they repeated that matters were not that simple, that he might himself be slain before he was a mile out of Port Bax, that he must be patient and wait until he came back to Sommerlund with the might of the Durenese army at his back.

Whenever they said this, he twisted his face in frustration. The worst of it was that he knew they were right. On his way to Hammerdal his life had been threatened by mortals and by spawn—and, he felt sure, by magic. Here he seemed to be safe, protected by a halo of magic which seemed to surround Hammerdal, but as soon as he left the city he would be at the mercy of the old man he had once seen circling among the moonswept clouds.

Each morning, more to take his mind off his enforced idleness than anything else, he exercised, wrestling with the strongest fighters whom Alin could lend him from his personal bodyguard. These mock duels became something of a regular fixture in the court's life. Young men and women would gather round on the lawn directly outside King Alin's gymnasium and watch as various of their friends struggled to see who could be the first to defeat Lone Wolf in unarmed combat. Since he had been united with the Sommerswerd he found that his body moved with a new grace and ease, as if he had the power of two people locked up inside a single form. Few of the people against whom he wrestled could contest with him for more than half a minute.

He was there one morning when he heard a familiar voice.

"Ho there, little brother. Showing off in front of these lilies, are we?"

"Viveka!"

She moved easily through the little crowd surrounding him, her scarred face smiling, her piercing eyes scattering the courtiers in front of her. She was shabbily dressed, and one arm hung uselessly by her side, but the trimness and economy of her movements made her seem to shine among the floral gaudiness of the high-bred men and women around her.

Lone Wolf absentmindedly threw his latest rival to the ground, winding the muscular youth so that he gasped on the fragrant lawn, and moved towards the mercenary, arms outstretched ready to fold her to him. In this place where everybody but nobody was a friend, the sight of Viveka's face was like sunlight to him.

At the last moment he paused, and offered her his hand. She shook it gravely, with her good hand, and he could feel the strength in her fingers.

"So you made it, big sister!"

" 'Course I did. I had to come and collect my fee, after all."

She clapped him on the shoulder. It was the heaviest blow anyone had inflicted on him all week, and he staggered slightly.

"I think you may have difficulty."

Her mercurial face was immediately scowling.

"What do you mean?"

"Well, big sister, you didn't actually protect me on my journey—"

"And who killed that priest—what was his name? Persimmon, or something. Who killed Persimmon and saved your life? You were hardly able to stand up at the time, as I recall, and he'd have had you for mincemeat if I hadn't been there!"

She had moved into a half-crouch, a wildcat ready to spring, her good hand at a dagger on her belt. The courtiers muttered uneasily, some of them choosing to drift away as if something of greater interest had just come to their attention. Lone Wolf wanted to laugh at Viveka and to hug her to him, but he knew that the mercenary's unpredictable temper might take this either way. After all, she had promised to be his friend only so long as it suited her, and if all prospects of receiving a fee were disappearing in front of her she might decide that it no longer suited her. Allied as he was with the Sommerswerd, he was fairly sure that he could defend himself against her—especially since she was effectively one-armed—but in so doing he might have to harm her or even kill her, and this was far from what he wanted to do.

Suddenly she chuckled and relaxed.

"You're a good lad, little brother. I'll take the matter up with that Sommlending king of yours. First of all I'll have to get to Sommerlund, of course, keeping an eye on you the while. You don't happen to know anyone who's going there soon, do you, so that I can beg a ride?"

"There's this army I've heard about, big sister. You could always join up."

"What? And be just another old sweat in the infantry? You have to be joking, brother!"

"Oh," he said airily, studiously looking at his fingers, "I don't think you'd have any chance of being enlisted in the infantry. The Durenese army have high standards, you know. One-armed soldiers are likely to be left at home, tilling the fields and earning themselves an honest . . . ouch!"

He doubled up over Viveka's hard fist, gasping, his eyes watering. Had it not been for the strength which he had gained from his union with the Sommerswerd, he would have been on the ground at her feet, choking from the unexpected punch. As it was, the muscles of his stomach already felt as if someone had hit them with a sledgehammer.

He reeled backwards, still folded over, and began to laugh through his pain.

"I accept it, I accept it, big sister!" he said, holding up his hand as if to ward off another blow. "Even single-handed you could beat all the Durenese infantry into a shapeless heap and still have time for breakfast."

"And quite right, too," said Viveka, looking at her knuckles in puzzled pain. "Has anyone ever told you you've got an exceptionally hard stomach?"

Lone Wolf moved his mind so that the ache was released from his muscles, and he stood up to his full height.

"A number of things have changed about me since we last met, big sister," he said gravely. "I'll tell you—but later, perhaps over a meal. For now, I want you to meet Madin and see if he and I together can do something about that arm of yours."

Madin was a wandering herbwarden, famous throughout all the Lastlands for his knowledge of the healing arts. As chance had had it, he had been in Hammerdal when Lone Wolf had arrived, and had worked with the young man to heal his physical and spiritual wounds through the use of potions and hours of silent meditation. He had, in addition, eased Lone Wolf's mind through the trauma of his fusion with the soul-stuff of the Sommerswerd. A couple of days before, his wise eyes sombre, he had told Lone Wolf that the body of Rhygar had been found, hideously mutilated, near the mouth of Tarnalin. Lone Wolf had accepted the news impassively; he had already known, in some way he couldn't precisely define, that Rhygar was dead.

Lone Wolf led Viveka around the bulge of the King's Tower to a side entrance. As they went she told him how the merchant Halvorc had died in the struggle with the Gorn Cove guards, but how Ganon and Dorier had finally been able to persuade the villagers of their innocence. The two knights had brought her with them to Port Bax, and from there she had travelled in the back of a woodman's wagon to Hammerdal, certain that she would find him at King Alin's court. She had used a few words of blandishment to persuade the palace guards to let her by—a fact which chilled Lone Wolf: for all they had known, she could have been a Helghast.

The Durenese were too accustomed to peace: such laxness could endanger their entire enterprise.

Troubled in his mind, he pushed open an arched pine door and ushered her in ahead of him. They were in a warm gloom, the air filled with the tangy, unidentifiable scents of the herbs which Madin had gathered. The old man himself appeared through the greyness almost immediately, smiling paternally at Lone Wolf and then looking with more interest at Viveka.

"A friend of yours?" he asked.

"So long as she chooses to be. Her arm—she injured it badly while saving my life."

Madin sat Viveka down on a crude wooden stool and pushed the sleeve of her tunic back to look at the inside of her elbow. He hissed as the lacerated, half-healed flesh came into view. Then he looked at Lone Wolf and nodded.

"Between my lore and your Kai powers," he said, "we can restore her arm to her. But it'll be a week before she can have the full use of it—maybe longer."

"Maybe shorter," said Viveka tersely. "The talk in Hammerdal is that the fleet will be ready to leave in five days, and I may have some fighting to do after that."

"Maybe shorter," Madin agreed, conciliatorily. "But you'll be lucky," he added under his breath, ignoring the sudden tightening of Viveka's lips as her sharp ears caught the words. "Now, let me find some root of laumspur, and we'll see what we can do."

Much later that day, Lone Wolf and Viveka sat side by side on a quilted couch. Her arm was wrapped from shoulder to wrist in creamy linen bandages, but she swore that already she could feel it healing. She had declined to shed her tattered clothing for the more ornate raiment of the court, although the servants assigned to her had begged her to do so, and Lone Wolf, inspired by her example, had discarded the overfussy garments he had been forcing himself to wear the last week or more, and had instead donned again his green cloak, jerkin and trousers.

These had been cleaned and repaired expertly, so that they seemed almost like new, and yet they wrapped themselves familiarly about his body. It seemed a long time since he had felt so fully at his ease.

There had been some tense moments during dinner. Axim and Viveka had recognized each other at once, and it was clear that there was no great love between them. The stately knight, jabbing his great hooked nose at the air expressively, had muttered about assassins and gutter-scum, whereas Viveka, smiling sweetly, had whispered in Lone Wolf's ear some remarks about Axim which had startled him with their graphic inventiveness and vividly pictorial language. Tomorrow . . . tomorrow he would have to bring the two of them together and try to patch up some sort of friendship between them; for the moment he was too relaxed, his stomach too full of good food and wine, to be concerned about it.

The gossip which Viveka had picked up in Hammerdal had been correct, as Lone Wolf had discovered during his evening conference with Axim and the king: in five days' time the Durenese fleet would sail for Sommerlund from Port Bax. From all over the country troops had been summoned, and a vast army was even now being drilled on the plains surrounding the city. The Helghast seemed to have fled Durenor as precipitously as they had arrived, for no longer did reports filter in to the capital of atrocities committed on outlying towns and villages; Lone Wolf was certain that they had gone to rejoin their master's army at Holmgard.

Musicians plucked carefully formal notes, and some of the courtiers danced in predetermined patterns across the floor, their finely woven clothes swaying as they moved. Now that Viveka was here, Lone Wolf saw the graceful men and women as nothing more than distracting decorations and heard the music as a tedious sequence of soul-less tinkling sounds.

He put his arm around Viveka's shoulder affectionately and, after a momentary pause, she nestled clumsily against his shoulder, protecting her injured limb.

"Five days, Viveka," he said. "It's not very long for your wound to heal."

"Long enough, little brother."

"Will you train with me? None of these callysparrows has given me a decent contest."

"If you feel strong enough to do battle with a one-armed woman, oh mighty warrior, I suppose I . . . "

He smiled, and her words drifted away to mix themselves up in the minstrels' music.

That night he escorted her to her room. His mind was pleasantly muzzy from the wine he had drunk; although he knew that he could clear away the warm haze at any moment, he chose deliberately not to.

At her door she stopped and turned to put one finger to his lips.

"Don't say it," she said.

"Say what?" he muttered.

"What you were going to say. I'm just your big sister, remember?"

"But—"

"No. Not a word. I know what you feel. It's as if there were only the two of us here, surrounded by all these other people who care more for the latest cut in clothing than for what really matters. That's *all* that you're feeling. Don't spoil things, little brother."

"Viveka, I—"

"Shut up."

She took his head and kissed him firmly on the forehead. Then she stood back, smiled frankly at him, and impulsively brushed his lips with her mouth.

The door slammed and she was gone.

2

Night. The flames of an eager fire lit up the inside of Zagarna's huge red war-tent, pitched on what had once been a stretch of pasture close by Holmgard, now a sea of mud churned up by countless taloned feet. The Darklord's colossal form lay spread upon a shrouded settle, his secondary mouth chewing eagerly on a human leg, his great blue flanks heaving and his eyes staring in mindless fury across the broad shelf of his face. Zagarna tried to shout his rage, but little could be heard except a soft bubbling noise, muted still further by the thick sphere of glass which encased his head.

We can speak better this way, thought Vonotar reprovingly.

You've failed me! The mouth in Zagarna's abdomen chewed even more avidly, as if somehow it could express more fully the Darklord's wrath.

It is no matter for concern.

The boy lives! You told me that you would see him die, and yet he lives! Don't you call that "failure"?

A temporary setback, my friend. Nothing more.

The sorcerer was seated in mid-air, apparently calm and collected. His eyes flamed a placid redness, occasionally flaring into yellow. In fact, he was more worried than it would have been wise ever to admit to the Darklord. A string of unlucky coincidences had thwarted his attempts to put an end to Lone Wolf's puny existence. Or were they coincidences? That was the trouble—he wasn't sure. Weeks had passed now since last he had sensed the presence of that other power, the entity who had taken away his youth from him. At times he suspected that she had left Magnamund forever, that she had decided for unknowable reasons of her own to cease tormenting him; for most of the time, though, he was uneasily aware that perhaps she was somewhere *out there*, ready and waiting to do battle with him once again. If only he could be confident, one way or the other, he would know what next to do!

But he shielded these doubts from the eyes and the mind of the Darklord.

Vonotar, Zagarna was thinking, *I find it hard to*

believe that a mere slip of a boy could have avoided you for so long—you who claim to have magical powers never before seen on this world! He reached out for another severed human limb, squashing it appreciatively in his clawed hands as he bore it to his lower mouth. *Wizard, I suspect you of treachery!*

Vonotar was accustomed to the Darklord's periodic furies and accusations. They made no impression on him any longer. Of course, Zagarna wasn't aware that he, Vonotar, had elected himself to be a fellow-Darklord. Indeed, if Vonotar had his way, Zagarna would die before ever that realization came to him. For the moment, though, he felt that it was in his interests to maintain their fragile alliance. But his patience, he knew, was rapidly evaporating . . .

Darklord, you know, for you can see into my thoughts, that I could never sustain any ideas of treason towards you. His eyes were momentarily blue, but he forced the colour to ebb back towards red again. *We have Holmgard at our feet, and within days it will be ours. Once their king has been burnt alive atop its highest parapet, the Sommlending will be like cowed dogs, anxious to obey our every whim. Surely you could never have come this far had it not been for my faithful assistance.* Vonotar let a sneer colour his thought. *My lord, you may have all the power of the Darkness, but only the magic that I can deploy could have brought us thus far. And you talk to me of treason! And of failure!*

Wizard, I do not like you.

There is no reason why we should like each other. But, for all that, we need each other. Is it not true?

Yes, yes, grumbled Zagarna resentfully, *I suppose it's true. But truth is the gallows upon which they hang the starving man. I have no wish to starve, nor to hang.*

And neither shall you. Soon—perhaps within the week— you will be standing four-square over all of Sommerlund, and not a warrior will dare to say your name except to praise it!

Zagarna absorbed this slowly, and for a while his thoughts were silent. He was fond of flattery, from whatever source. The idea of his final triumph over the hated foe was a sweet one, and he relished it slowly as he swallowed it into the cavernous maw of his mind.

But still, he thought finally, grudgingly, *there is the matter of the boy.*

I shouldn't think that he will trouble us for long, Vonotar countered immediately. *Within a few short days, he and a vast army from Durenor will be setting sail for these shores—*

Wizard! You never told me this! The Darklord sat up, his limbs moving restlessly, cutting through the air, wishing that it were flesh that they flayed.

I didn't tell you because it isn't important to you! The harshness of Vonotar's thought cracked across the air between them. *Once they are at sea they are at my mercy! I can doom the boy and the Durenese scum as one!*

And how do you propose to do this, wizard?

By taking an idea, and moulding it until it is in the shape that I desire, and then allowing it to fly loose in the skies above the Holmgulf.

Vonotar's ancient face cracked into a calculated smile.

I'm fed up with your riddles, wizard! Tell me in plain words that I can understand!

So Vonotar told Zagarna as much of his plan as he thought it likely that the Darklord could understand.

3

The brassy blare of a thousand trumpets was still in Lone Wolf's ears as Port Bax slowly disappeared on the eastern horizon. All around him the world was filled with the creaking of timbers, the calls of sailors, the splashing of waves as wooden hulls cut weightily through them, the hoarse cries of sea-birds, the slap of sails as they took the wind. He was at sea again, the spiced air stinging in his nostrils as he breathed.

Beside him Viveka moved smoothly, like him leaning with her arms on the rail surrounding the fo'c'sle. Nearby

Lord Axim was standing rigidly, staring out to sea ahead of them; he and Viveka, at the instigation of Lone Wolf, had entered into a hesitant truce—at least for the duration of the war. It had emerged that the mercenary had been responsible for the death of one of Lord Axim's kin, a murder which she now barely remembered, having performed it years ago for some forgotten client, who had paid her well but who otherwise had made not the slightest impression on her memory. (Or, at least, that was what she claimed. Lone Wolf suspected, from her openness and frankness on the matter, that she remembered only too clearly who her paymaster had been, but was holding to her contract by confiding the person's name to no one.) The two of them maintained a stiff politeness in each other's company—which, Lone Wolf accepted, was as much as he could expect from them.

He remembered the last time he had been upon these waters, first aboard the *Green Sceptre*, then adrift in the angry iciness, and then in the ramshackle confines of the fishing vessel. Now he stood near the bows of the greatest of all Durenor's warships—a craft herself called the *Durenor*, in recognition of her pre-eminence. She was perhaps a hundred and fifty feet from stem to stern, with a great curving prow and three tall masts that seemed almost to scratch against the clouds. She carved through the waters remorselessly, her every movement declaring her strength. Behind her, scattered out across the broad cloth of the sea, were spread more than fifty others of the mightiest galleons at Durenor's command, each bearing a small army of skilled warriors. Ten thousand of the finest soldiers of all Durenor were aboard this fleet; ten thousand men and women who had vowed that they would have vengeance on the hordes of the Darklord, or that they would give up their lives in the attempt.

Lone Wolf's mind went back to the tiny fishing vessel and the petty criminals who had formed its crew. *They meant to kill me,* he thought, *and for a while I was in their power. How things have changed . . .*

His hand moved briefly to the hilt of the Sommerswerd, brushing it with his fingertips as he did so frequently that now he barely noticed what he was doing. At every contact he and the sword exchanged a little of their soul-stuff, further cementing the bond between them. He felt now as if there were no clear demarcation that divided himself from the weapon.

A bell chimed. It was midday, time for them to eat.

This they did at the captain's table. The commander of all the fleet, and the captain of the *Durenor*, was a slight man with a twisted, withered leg—exactly the opposite of what Lone Wolf had always imagined an admiral should look like. He was already seated at his table when they arrived, and he gestured towards the other seats, a gleam of welcome in his shrewd eyes.

"The winds seem set well for us, Admiral Calfen," said Axim, waiting, his hand on the back of his chair, while Viveka seated herself. Hatred for her might be simmering just below the surface, but still, in the manner of the Durenese military aristocracy, he extended her every courtesy.

"Aye," said the admiral. "This time of year, the winds should be with us all the way to the Holmgulf, Ishir be willing."

"How long will it take us to reach Holmgard?" Lone Wolf asked. Although he already knew the answer, he knew also that time was desperately tight; he prayed that Calfen would have good news for him. Already thirty-three days of his mission had gone by, and Ulnar had warned him that Holmgard could hold out against the Darklord's siege for no more than forty.

"Three days, maybe four," said the admiral, smiling sympathetically at the young Kai. "There's no way that we can make the ships travel faster than they want to, and that's a fact."

The answer was the same as before. Lone Wolf looked gloomy.

"But if there's nothing we can do to change these things, then where's the sense in worrying about 'em?" said the admiral complacently, looking with unabashed interest at a bowl of meat broth that had been placed in front of him.

"This tastes good," remarked Viveka, who had ignored ceremony and simply pitched straight in. Axim looked at her and visibly controlled a shudder.

Skilfully Calfen steered the conversation towards other things, and the meal passed without incident.

As, indeed, did the succeeding days, although all of them became more and more imbued by the feeling that there was something desperately wrong. It seemed as if there was a creeping malaise upon the fleet, as if something was sucking the spirit out of the crews and the warriors. Whereas at first cries of greeting, often ribald and derogatory, had been passed regularly and cheerfully between the galleons whenever they moved close to each other, now the more usual response was a moody silence, or at best a formal exchange of information. Aboard their own ship, the *Durenor*, the soldiers who had only a couple of days before been eager to volunteer to help or to exchange a witticism were now a sullen, broody lot, forgetful of their clothing and the condition of their weapons, staring towards the west with slack-jawed dread.

Viveka was the first to broach the subject at the captain's table, on the evening of their third day.

"Your soldiers are poor sailors, Lord Axim," she observed mildly, picking her teeth fastidiously.

The hooked nose pointed towards her like an offensive weapon, and the Durenese aristocrat's hard eyes stared down it at her. He made as if to speak, but instead just snarled, low in his throat.

Viveka carried on lightly, as if she had heard nothing. "But then your sailors don't seem to be very good sailors, either, do they, Admiral Calfen? All of them would appear to have been made just as queasy by the waves as my Lord's soldiers."

The old seafarer just looked at her. There was no real animus in his gaze, just a paternal exasperation. Then his face changed.

"You're right, Viveka," he said suddenly. "We can't just make things go away by refusing to talk about them. Something's draining our people as if they were sponges being sucked dry. I don't like it, no I don't. It smacks to me of magic, and not the magic of good, either."

Now that Calfen had spoken it was as if he had burst open a dam in Axim's reserve. The warrior began to speak, and the words came gushing out of him.

"Now that you say it, Calfen, my friend, I, too, have felt a touch of whatever vile force it is that's sapping the strength of our men and women. It's like walking close to the edge of a cliff and feeling it drawing you towards it. You know it would be madness to go any closer to it, and yet still it pulls at you, as if it were speaking directly to your mind. And by the time you force yourself to turn and walk away from it, to force it out of your mind, you feel as if it had pulled half of your soul away with it."

"It hasn't affected me," said Viveka. For once her remark to the lord wasn't deliberately barbed; she was looking straight at him, her eyes serious, her forehead lined with sincere curiosity.

"Nor me," Lone Wolf put in. "But then," he added, "I bear the Sommerswerd."

Viveka smiled somewhat bitterly at him.

"Lucky little fellow, aren't you, little brother?" she said softly.

Lone Wolf looked startled. He'd intended it as nothing more than a statement of fact.

"But you say you've felt nothing of it," said Axim leaning forwards earnestly. "Now, I wonder why that could be?"

"I don't know," said Viveka very slowly, pacing the syllables deliberately. "If I knew, I swear I would tell you."

Perhaps you, too, have breathed the breath of the nameless ones, he thought, but he said nothing of this.

Calfen was looking at him.

"But as you say, young Kai Lord, there's a perfectly rational explanation for your own escape from this evil influence. You are shielded from it by the Sommerswerd at your hip. Is there no way, perhaps, that the Sommerswerd could shield us all? Because, if this goes on, it'll be hardly worth our sailing into the Holmgulf. Our people will just take one look at the Darklord's army and run away screaming, they will."

Viveka put her hand to her mouth and giggled artificially. Both of the older men gave her a filthy look.

Axim's temper deserted him and he spat out savage words: "It's nothing to laugh about, you she-cat from the sliming pits of—"

Lone Wolf cut in quickly.

"I don't know if I can call upon the Sommerswerd to aid us all, Admiral," he said pointedly. "I'll go right now to my cabin and see if I can blend my own poor powers with those of the sword. Failing that—well, who are we to be able to counter magic?"

He left the three of them heatedly discussing what would be their best tactic if, indeed, they landed in Holmgard with an army that was still demoralized and dispirited into uselessness. Lone Wolf was pleased to notice two things as he went. First, the dangerous rift that had opened up between Viveka and Axim had closed almost as suddenly as it had appeared, and the two of them were cooperating fully in the conference. Second, they were all talking in terms of what should be done if Lone Wolf's attempts to lift the curse should still be unsuccessful by the time they reached Holmgard: it seemed not to have occurred to any of them that there was always the alternative of simply turning round and heading back to Port Bax. Lone Wolf's heart warmed towards all three of them.

In his cramped cabin he reverently laid the Sommerswerd on his bunk, and looked at it, his mind heavy with concern. It glowed less brightly when it was not at his belt or in his hand—its light was merely a red warmth, now. He had always felt uneasy about the forces of magic: he had accepted that, in the right hands, they could be used to effect great things, but at the same time the very thought of them filled him with distrust. Whose were the "right hands"? He knew that there were disciples of the magic of Evil employed by the Darklords in their fastnesses beyond the Durncrag Mountains, and he had little doubt that some of them had come with the conquering army. Were *theirs* the "right hands"? No, of course not! And then there were magicians who meant well, but who were unable to control the powers at their disposal. He thought of the nursery fables his mother had told him about such magicians, when he had been an infant at her knee. And he thought, too, of the young weakling of a trainee enchanter he had met so soon after the destruction of the Kai Monastery. Were *theirs* the "right hands," either? Again, certainly not. Inept magicians were, if anything, even more dangerous than evil ones.

He shook his head sadly.

Yet it seemed that, despite all his doubts, now that he bore the Sommerswerd he, too, would have to dabble in the occult arts. To be sure, some of the Kai abilities and senses were so close to magic that it was hard to distinguish them from the real thing; but that was . . . *different*. He couldn't think why, for a moment, but his mind was shouting at him that this was the case. And then he had it: the Kai abilities were nascent within everyone, and were thus merely a natural manifestation of human beings. Magic was drawn from outside the individual; it was something extra, which people had to bring into themselves. You trained to *turn yourself into* a magician; whereas you trained as a Kai in order to *let yourself become what you already really were*. That was the difference. That was why he welcomed every sign in himself of the one and was so profoundly suspicious of the other.

His own Kai abilities, however, were as yet far from fully developed. He didn't know if they were up to bonding with the soul-stuff of the Sommerswerd in order to repel the magical assault upon the fleet.

He stared at the sword. It was untold thousands of years old. It had been held in the great hand of King Ulnar I when he had slain the Darklord Vashna at the Maakengorge. It must have encountered magic on this scale before. Surely at least some of the earlier Sommlending who had borne the weapon had united their souls with it to drive off evils as pervasive and insinuating as this one?

He knelt down and touched the palms of his hands to the blade of the Sommerswerd, his other self, and he opened his mind to it completely.

For a moment he felt nothing but a stillness of such profound tranquillity that it was as if he had no senses, no real being.

And then his body was electrified with power, every cell singing with energies created in the time when the Lastlands themselves had been children. He was plunging down through the waters of the ocean, screaming with exultation. Down he went through the sea-bed, scattering corals and the oozes of the millennia, thrusting aside the brittle rocks of the world's crust, darting unimpeded into the molten rock beneath. He bathed in the boiling heat for a fraction of a second, and then continued his flight downward, downward and ever downward. Great igneous masses, lancing bright red and searing white, rolled towards him—but he drove on straight through them, laughing maniacally at their discomfiture. He saw the curving lines of magnetism like dark wires within the magma, but every time he approached them they shrank away, flinching from his touch. The tormented liquid rock could offer him no more resistance than if he were pushing his hand into

135

cream. Now the light was even more intense, so that the magma seemed as if it were straining against the pressure of the world above to explode outwards in a triumphant flare of brilliance and destruction. And then the light grew dimmer, as the weight of all Magnamund cowed the fiery spirits of the rock, forcing it into stillness.

He burst through into a new region, and he knew that he was close to the heart of the world. He was piercing through liquid metal that was so hot that the word "heat" no longer had any meaning, and yet he felt its touch as coolness. He whooped in exhilaration as he came nearer and nearer to the very core of Magnamund. He was temporarily crazed—he knew it, and he rejoiced in his madness.

And then he was standing by the edge of a pond, a fishing-rod in his hands. He had been here all the long day, and now the sun was sinking towards the west. He had caught enough of the fat fish that lived in this pond for his family to have plenty for supper, plus a couple to be salted and stored away. Perhaps another cast or two across the placid water before he packed his creel away and set out over the curve of the hill for home? Well, just another one . . .

He raised the rod behind his head.

There was another shadow, besides his own, on the surface of the water. He turned, incuriously, to see who this fellow-angler might be. He hadn't noticed him earlier, so presumably the man had come down in the late afternoon to chance his luck with a cast or two.

The man was dressed in a robe of blue, upon which were embroidered stars of silver.

He felt Lone Wolf's gaze upon him, for he turned and smiled a wintry smile.

"You!"

"Yes, Lone Wolf, it's me. You saw me sailing close to the moon when the *Green Sceptre* went down, and I thought you had been swallowed by the ocean. If you'd known where to look, you would have seen me watching at other times—when that fool of a priest of mine tried to use his clumsy poison on you, or when you were attacked back in that tavern in Holmgard."

The angler tittered.

"The Darklord's Helghast should have taken you in Tarnalin, of course, and for long enough I assumed they'd done so, but when I returned to gloat over the rags of your body I found that the fools had failed: they were destroyed most cruelly, I can assure you. As indeed was your friend—that bluff, stolid and incredibly stupid man Rhygar: I took great joy in subjecting him to all the tortures I wished to exact on you, Lone Wolf, and he was screaming to be spared as he died."

"I don't believe you! Rhygar would never have—"

"Oh, but he did. You'd better take my word for it—after all, I'm the only one who was there . . . apart from Rhygar, that is, and of course he won't be telling you. Now, just wait a moment, I think I saw a fish rise."

The ancient man cast his line, and for a while seemed to concentrate on it entirely. However, the cast was unsuccessful, and wearily he drew in his line.

"We're both fishers, you and I, Lone Wolf," he said reflectively. "You put out your line, hoping that it'll be taken by something good, and all that seems to happen is that the fish die before you can ever haul them up to the shore. Me? I throw out my lines as well, but what I seek are living fish who will obey my will in everything. I've caught quite a few such fish now, you know, some of them very big fish indeed. And they do what I tell them to do."

Lone Wolf could see that the man's back was unnaturally bent with age. Wispy white hairs were plastered to his pallid forehead. His eyes were empty as he turned away from the pond to look at Lone Wolf.

"You died, you know," he said. "I saw you die. You died when a fisherman cut away your throat with his knife, and your life bled away on the unvarnished deck of the sorry vessel he thought himself proud to command. I watched as the life was leeched away from you, and yet later I found that you were still alive. Tell me—it's merely a matter of curiosity on my part—how did that come to happen?"

Lone Wolf cast his own line, even though it was by now far too late and his mother would be beginning to wonder where he had got to.

"I don't remember dying," he said. "I think perhaps that I might—if I had."

"But you did," said the ancient man vexedly. "I can assure you most readily that you did. Lone Wolf—the last of the Kai—that was it: dead."

He knifed his hand through the air descriptively.

"You're mad! I'm here. Look at me. I'm alive!"

"And so you are—*here*. But of course 'here' isn't anywhere that you might expect it to be. 'Here' is somewhere that your mind and mine have conjured up between them. You can't say that it really exists."

"But up there"—Lone Wolf pointed with his thumb—"there is reality, and I'm still alive in that reality. Wizard, sorcerer, whoever you are—remember that there is always such a thing as the present."

"There is indeed."

The bent old man crumpled up his fishing-rod, looking almost ruefully at the splintered pieces that were left in his hands.

"If you want, Lone Wolf, you can dismiss all this as a dream." He threw away the pieces of his rod, and they floated on the surface of the pond. "But I don't think that you will. It makes no difference. You have defied all of the adversaries that I have sent against you, but on our next encounter you will have to deal with me myself. That will be something different, will it not?"

"Yes," said Lone Wolf, his voice subdued, "something very different."

The ancient man seemed content with his empty creel,

for he hefted it easily up on one elbow. His shoes—far too light for exploring the banks of a pond—seemed not to touch the mud as he turned away.

"Let me ask you something," said Lone Wolf. He was very conscious of the fact that it was the first positive move that he had made since coming here, despite the proud shout of his descent.

"Ask away."

"I've seen you before—you said as much yourself. But who *are* you?"

"Oh." The ancient man seemed for a moment surprised, and then he regained his poise on the crumbling bank. "I would have thought that was something you knew by now."

"I don't."

"Hmmm. You really are a very poorly informed young man, you know. It'll be something that you can think about when you meet your death in the Holmgulf, as the Durenese cry out their piteous whines all around you. I shouldn't think that it will make too much difference, now, if I tell you who I am."

The angler paused, his rod sloped over the shoulder of his star-studded blue robe.

"My name is Vonotar. It is the name of the nemesis of the Lastlands. Is that enough to satisfy your query?"

4

Vonotar shuffled uneasily in his bed. On the other side of this bare stone cell in Kaag, Carag snored lustily. Vonotar felt as if something had been stolen from his mind, but he didn't know what it was. He tried to throw himself further into sleep, but the uncanny light of the walls of Kaag projected itself through the lids of his eyes. He whimpered like a child, pulling the bedclothes more closely about him.

5

Lone Wolf burst back into the captain's cabin. Calfen, Axim and Viveka were still seated there; Axim, Lone Wolf realized astonishedly, was drunk. In front of him there was a mess of empty wine-bottles, and his fist beat repeatedly upon the table.

"Silence!" Lone Wolf shouted.

Calfen and Viveka turned and stared; Axim gazed at him owlishly. Lone Wolf swiftly explained what had happened.

"I've been told the truth," he said. "The Sommerswerd helped me discover it. We were right—our troops are being weakened by magic. I even know who's creating the malicious spell. But our people aren't being softened up for when we reach Holmgard. The sorcerer—Vonotar—plans to strike at us even before we get there. He's going to attack while we're in the Holmgulf!"

"Tomorrow," said Calfen listlessly.

Viveka looked at Lone Wolf with her disconcertingly acute eyes.

"How's he going to attack us?" she said.

"I don't know."

"Anyway, who *is* this Vonotar?"

"That's another thing I don't know. When I saw him—dreamed him, call it what you will—he was dressed in the costume of the Brotherhood of the Crystal Star."

"So even they would turn against Sommerlund, would they?" said Viveka thoughtfully, toying with a fork.

"Nonsense!" Axim shouted. "They'd never—"

"But they might," said Calfen cautiously, although it was clear that he didn't much like the idea.

"No, they wouldn't," Lone Wolf said. "I've met the weakest of all their number, and even he couldn't have been tempted into fighting for the forces of Evil. This . . . this Vonotar must be some kind of a renegade— or else maybe he was simply disguising himself in the Brotherhood's robes."

"Whoever he is, he's a very powerful sorcerer indeed," muttered Calfen. "I've heard a little of the ways of left-handed magic, and I know that it would take one of the greatest of all magicians to cast a spell like this one."

"Then indeed Vonotar must be one of the greatest of all magicians," Lone Wolf exploded. He told them tersely how he had been hounded by ill-luck ever since leaving Holmgard, and how it had been created by the ancient man.

"Might as well give up," said Axim sadly. "There's no way we can compete with magic as powerful as that."

"Don't be a fool," said Viveka suddenly. "Don't talk of giving up! That's exactly what Vonotar wants you to do. You've been touched by his damned spell. You'd never think of giving up, otherwise."

She took Lone Wolf's agreement for granted, but looked backwards and forwards between Axim and Calfen, her eyes challenging them. Neither of the two men could find anything to say.

"Right then," Viveka concluded, pouring herself another glass of wine, "we're all agreed that we keep sailing on towards the Holmgulf. And we look forward with pleasure and delight to the prospect of a merry battle on the morrow, do we not?"

The two older men agreed hesitantly. Lone Wolf searched on the table for a clean glass, found one, filled it and touched it to Viveka's.

"A toast!" he cried. "A toast to our victory tomorrow!"

He and Viveka raised their glasses, their eyes meeting. Axim and Calfen assented half-heartedly.

"To victory," they murmured. But neither of them raised a glass.

141

6

It could have been the toast or it could have been his encounter with Vonotar, but whatever the reason the shroud of gloom and despondency had lifted from the fleet by the following morning.

Lone Wolf woke to the sound of crewmen hurling good-natured abuse at each other, and he knew from the timbre of their oaths that things were back to normal again. He turned over in his bunk; it was not particularly comfortable, but he was reluctant to leave its warmth. He pushed his head firmly into the hard, slightly damp-smelling pillow and closed his eyes tightly against the flood of daylight streaming in through the porthole. Today, he knew, was going to be a grim one: Vonotar had promised him as much. There was the possibility that he might lose his life, although this he discounted: someone or something had been protecting him over the past few weeks, he knew from speaking with the sorcerer, and presumably that same agency would continue to do so. But there was little point in his own personal survival if he failed to reach Holmgard in time to save the city— and the whole nation of Sommerlund. He dreaded the thought of failure even more than he dreaded the chance of his own death.

A few tumbled, half-dreaming thoughts went through his mind, and he tried to persuade himself that he was really still asleep.

But it was no use: the day refused to be denied.

He rolled out of his bunk and searched around the floor for his clothes. He splashed some cold water on his face, but didn't bother with any more washing than that. He shook his head vigorously, so that droplets of water sprayed everywhere; the rapid movement brought him fully awake.

Axim, Calfen and Viveka were already on deck when he got there, the wiry admiral with a telescope to his eye.

"Don't like the look of that," he was saying to the other two. "Don't like the look of it at all." His dourness was in contrast to the good cheer of the others.

"A fine good morning to you!" said Lone Wolf. Viveka had cued him last night to the fact that one of their best defences against whatever the day might bring was to adopt a pose of gaiety.

"Morning!" said Axim brightly. "Sleep well?"

"Like a top. And you, Viveka?"

"I slept well, thank you, little brother."

"Calfen?"

"Shut up and take a look at this."

Lone Wolf took the telescope and held it up to his eye. As he did so he felt his mask of cheerfulness slip. The brightness of the day dimmed into a sorry grey, and his shoulders bent as if they were burdened by a heavy load.

"Well, look through it, can't you?" snapped the admiral.

Leadenly Lone Wolf did so. Directly ahead of them was Wreck Point, the southernmost tip of the Kirlundin Isles. But the cruelly jagged rocks of the headland were obscured from his view. A fog seemed to be emanating from Wreck Point and rolling across the surface of the sea; Lone Wolf was reminded of a troupe of dancers spreading themselves on the stage before starting their performance. The feeling of dismal hopelessness seeped into him.

"It's just a fog," he said dully, passing the telescope to Viveka.

As he did so, he felt the gloom lift. He struck the telescope out of her hands, so that it went twisting and turning over the side of the *Durenor* to splash in the water.

Calfen knotted a fist. The small man looked as if he were about to attack Lone Wolf, but . . .

"No!" Viveka shouted. "I felt it, too. There was something in the telescope. It was *making* us feel despondent. Lone Wolf was right to get rid of it."

"Yes, friend," said Axim slowly, putting a restraining arm on the admiral's shoulder. "There was evil magic in that telescope. I, too, experienced it a while ago, but I thought it was just the dolour of the day."

Calfen's fury subsided. "Aye, and that may be so, it may be so," he said. He spat over the rail into the churning water. "But there's still the fog."

They looked ahead and, sure enough, Calfen was right: the fog had erected itself over the sea like a drystone wall, and it was directly in their path. It seemed to stretch all the way from the surface of the ocean to the frontiers of the heavens. It was massive and solid, unchanging and implacable.

But wait. There was movement within it. Against the grey of the uncanny mist they could see dark shapes. At first they couldn't interpret what they saw: the patterns were abstract. Then the shapes gathered greater definition.

Calfen was the first of them to realize what was happening.

"Warships!" he bawled. "Warships ahead of us!"

"Prepare for battle," a crewman cried from the crow's nest. The shout was taken up by others among the fleet.

"So Vonotar attacks early," muttered Lone Wolf. "But I thought he'd have used a little more subtlety than this."

"And so would I," said Viveka, picking up his words. "Still, we have to fight him on his own grounds, and who are we to complain?"

The response of the soldiers to the call to battle was much more enthusiastic; they'd been cooped up in the ships for several days now. One of them started a cheer, and soon it was picked up by the others.

"I wish I could feel as excited as they do," said Lone Wolf to Viveka.

"It's just a question of killing more of them than they kill of us," she replied matter-of-factly. "Won't take long. Then we can carry on to this Holmgard of yours."

"I wish I had your . . . your coldness."

"You forget, little brother, that I've killed a lot of people in my time. A few more isn't going to make too much difference."

The enemy ships were closing on them rapidly, and as they did so a howl of dismay went up from the *Durenor*'s

144

crew, almost drowning out the martial cheering and yelling of the soldiers. Viveka and Lone Wolf looked at each other, startled,—what was happening to the sailors?

Calfen rushed past them, his face white and horrified.

"A nightmare!" he shouted as he went. "Every seam
. . . seam . . . sailor's nightmare!" His control over his speech was slipping.

Axim was at Lone Wolf's side.

"Look at them!" he hissed, his great nose stabbing towards the oncoming ships.

Lone Wolf looked—and flinched with horror.

The ships were black and water-stained. Here a mast was broken, there a hole gaped in a once-proud hull. Dredged up from the depths of the oceans by Vonotar's magic, these were the ships that had sunk over the centuries in the Holmgulf.

And they were manned by their original crews.

Lone Wolf sharpened the focus of his eyes, the way he had learned how to do in Tarnalin, and he saw, swarming among the rigging, moving slowly and laboriously, some missing limbs or even their heads, the sailors who had perished with their ships. Their rotted faces were twisted into masks of implacable hatred as they came towards the Durenese fleet.

A cold wind suddenly tugged at Lone Wolf, blasting across the sea like a rushing hurricane. As soon as it had come it was gone, and it swept away with it the unnatural silvery fog.

The wailing of the crews around them intensified, and Lone Wolf's heart quailed.

"There are thousands of them," Viveka breathed in his ear. It was the first time that he had known her to show any trace of fear—and that she was doing so now added to his own terror.

From side to side, ranged right across the width of the Holmgulf, stretched the carcases of the dead vessels, moving ponderously on the choppy waters. Even at this distance Lone Wolf could hear the moaning and

145

groaning of their tormented timbers.

Coming straight towards the *Durenor*, its wet sails taut against the sky, was the flagship of the fleet of the dead. It was a huge vessel, and from its vast prow extended a great clawed ram.

The two ships closed with uncanny speed.

Lone Wolf drew the Sommerswerd from its scabbard, and the blade cast its light on the deck around him. Viveka was scrambling up on the rail, a dagger in her teeth and her own sword drawn, preparing to leap aboard the oncoming vessel. Lone Wolf moved to follow her, but then the ram struck the *Durenor*'s hull, and he was thrown to one side, the splintering of boards and the screams of the crew filling his ears until he thought he would be deafened. He had no idea where Viveka and Axim could have got to; as soon as he had regained his balance he looked around for them but they were nowhere to be seen. The deck beneath his feet was canted over at an angle, and he knew that the ship must be taking on water—too much water: she must go down within minutes.

"Abandon ship!" screamed Calfen. Lone Wolf could only hear him; the little admiral must be somewhere behind him. "Abandon ship!"

Lone Wolf sheathed the Sommerswerd, leapt up on the guardrail, teetered there precariously for a moment, and then leaped precipitously forward towards the water-blackened deck of the flagship of the dead.

7

The rotting timbers held his weight only for a second and then they gave way, so that he went crashing through to the deck beneath. The sharp edges of the wood scraped at his face and hands, and he bruised the small of his back painfully on landing, but otherwise he was unhurt. All around him the timbers of the ship glowed with a cold grey phosphorescence, and the stench of decay choked him so that he retched drily, clutching his knotted stomach. As soon as he had recovered himself he staggered to his feet and drew the Sommerswerd from its jewelled scabbard. The sword in his hand shone with a great golden light, and he could see that he was in what must once have been the ship's main dining salon. Dank black seaweeds and small, sickly grey molluscs encrusted every surface. Shattered chairs and tables were tumbled together in chaos. A dead squid was wedged tightly under the decaying remains of the master table. The air was filled with the eerie creaking of the ship, and from the hole in the deck above him he could hear the screams and shouts of battle.

There was another noise.

It came from behind him, and he whirled around, the Sommerswerd at the ready. Lumbering uncertainly forwards, armed with huge rusted cutlasses, were four of this dead ship's crew. They were almost naked, their decomposing bodies covered only with tatters of wet clothing. Their faces were racked with pain, their empty eye-sockets swivelling towards him, seeing him with eyes which had long since been stolen by the sea's salt waters.

Suddenly Lone Wolf realized why the walking dead bore such hatred for the living. *They're in agony!* he thought wildly, cleaving the air in front of him with the Sommerswerd. *Vonotar has made them walk again, but they have to bear all the pain of their deaths. They must kill us all before he will release them to oblivion.*

A gargling cry of loathing ripped itself from the throat of one of the undead, and he clumsily ran towards Lone Wolf, his cutlass raised high above his head.

Lone Wolf stepped easily to one side, and with a great sweeping arc of the Sommerswerd cut the zombie in two at the waist. He was half-turned, ready to do battle with the other three, when some instinct made him glance back.

The . . . the *thing* was still alive. Rotting intestines spilling from its belly, the torso was still groping towards his ankles, pulling itself along the slimy, waterlogged

boards with one hand and jerkily swinging its cutlass
with the other.

Lone Wolf let out a scream of revulsion and took
one involuntary step backwards. Then he jumped swiftly towards the thing on the floor and swept down the
Sommerswerd to hack away the bloated hand clutching
the cutlass. The thing gave a bubbling shriek of frustration and tried to bite at him with its toothless, lipless
mouth. Lone Wolf kicked out at it, and the disintegrating
torso shot across the slippery deck to wrap itself against
the corpse of the squid. There it lay, still yelling its
incoherent fury.

Lone Wolf turned towards the other three—and not a
moment too soon, for they were almost upon him. The
blade of the Sommerswerd streaked through the air, deftly removing one zombie's fighting arm at the elbow. The
thing stopped in its tracks, still waving the stump of its
arm confusedly; clearly it didn't know what to do now
that its cutlass-arm was gone, and Lone Wolf felt a sudden wash of sympathy mingling with his horror.

*I must stop thinking of these things as people—it's slowing
me down. They're objects. Nothing but dangerous objects to
be got rid of.*

Two more swishes of the Sommerswerd, and all three
of the zombies were now incapacitated, snarling in a thin
watery frenzy of frustration at him but making no further
moves to attack.

He backed away from them, looking from side to
side, desperately searching for some way to get out of
this stinking room. He rested one hand on the slithery
surface of the master table, and saw that there was a door
at the end of the salon, its wood swollen and bloated so
that it filled its frame tightly. Ishir knew where it led to,
but it had to be somewhere better than this place.

Something clutched his ankle.

He yelped with fear, and looked down.

The hideously shattered carcase of the first zombie had
inched towards him. It was gripping his left boot tightly

148

with its remaining hand, and its face was turned up, tortured into a rictus of abomination.

Lone Wolf screamed again, and instinctively slashed out with the Sommerswerd. The blade scythed down through the thing's head and breastbone, shattering its ribs and releasing a sickening smell of corruption and decay. Lone Wolf gagged and tried to step away. He did so only with difficulty. The creature's hand was still locked to his foot, so that as he moved he dragged much of the mangled torso with him. There was the sharp, sour taste of vomit in his mouth. He stabbed with the sword, severing the grey arm at the wrist. Still the hand gripped him, but there was nothing he could do about it. Later, once he had got away from this vile place, he could chop it away with a dagger.

He turned and half-slid, half-ran towards the door he had spotted.

He had nearly reached it when he heard a low cackle from beyond. Something was moving there, and he sensed a great evil. He looked back at the hole he had made when he had fallen into this room, but there was no time to make his escape that way. Besides, he didn't think he could stomach passing the heap of limbs and organs littered across the deck beside the squid.

With luck the thing beyond the door would pass on by. No. He sensed that it knew he was here, and that it was waiting to burst through the door towards him.

He noticed rather than felt a strange tingling sensation around the fringes of his mind. It puzzled him for a moment, and then he recognized what was happening. Something—it must be the creature on the other side of the door—was trying to attack him mentally. Now that his soul-stuff had melded with the Sommerswerd's he was immune from the pain, but of course the creature couldn't know this.

He stood there, panting hoarsely, half-crouched ready to defend himself, both hands on the great hilt of the Sommerswerd.

The creature on the far side of the door seemed less certain of itself now. Its movements were even more furtive and cautious than before.

Lone Wolf's muscles were aching from the tension in which he was holding his body. He knew he didn't dare risk relaxing them. The creature might sense it, and choose that moment to attack.

Then suddenly the swollen door exploded towards him.

He forced himself not to flinch as shards of soft, decayed, pulpy wood showered around him.

Howling its hatred, a Helghast ran directly towards him, its evil black sword whistling straight for his neck.

He stood his ground, the Sommerswerd's golden blade held rigidly out in front of him.

The Helghast impaled itself through the chest and let out a high scream of agony. Lone Wolf twisted the blade, and ichor spurted from the wound. The Helghast screamed again, and staggered back, drawing itself clear of the Sommerswerd. It was moving unsteadily, whimpering in a mewl of pain, but its sword arm still moved purposefully. It looked Lone Wolf straight in the eyes. He returned the stare: it was like looking into the nightmarish depths of some infernal pit.

He forced his gaze away. The thing was trying to ensnare him with those vilely soulless eyes.

The Helghast snorted with fury as soon as it realized that he had freed his mind from its hypnotic hold, and then darted towards him once again.

This time Lone Wolf was not so well prepared, and the black blade sung through the air directly in front of his mouth. He jerked his head back and swept the Sommerswerd round in front of him with all the force he could muster.

It was a lucky blow, chopping straight into the spawn's side right through to the backbone.

The Helghast gave out one final, ear-shattering scream of pain, and then it was gone as if it had never been there.

Lone Wolf was stunned by the shock of the sudden disappearance, but he forced his unwilling feet to take him through the space where the Helghast had been, towards the empty frame of the door.

He found a rotting companionway, and nervously clambered up it to find himself on the topdeck. Everywhere he could see, men and women were battling the walking dead—the scene was a maelstrom of movement. The water around the ship was patterned with the floating remains of the undead, some of them still moving convulsively as if they were even now engaged in combat. A zombie lurched towards Lone Wolf and he reflexively hacked its head from its shoulders. It still tried to advance, weaving a bloodstained dagger in front of it, but he pushed at its breast with the tip of the Sommerswerd and it fell over backwards.

The Durenese seemed to be having the better of the fray. Some of the soldiers had discovered as Lone Wolf had below, that the undead could be put out of action by hacking away their weapon-arms. However, ancient arrows from a nearby vessel were hailing down on the deck, and many of the Durenese were falling under the deadly shower.

Suddenly there was a flash brighter than the sun. A ball of fire exploded from a tower at the stern of the flagship. It billowed out towards one of the Durenese vessels, and within seconds the wooden superstructure was a mass of flame. The men and women there screamed in horror and agony and, as Lone Wolf watched, many of them hurled themselves from the deck into the waters below, their clothes and hair blazing.

Lone Wolf's eyes narrowed. Vonotar's forces must have a mighty war engine of some kind concealed in that turret. He shuddered. He had never heard of any weapon capable of hurling fire the way that this one did. He suspected that it must employ dark magic.

He turned and made his way along the deck, moving cautiously, ever wary of attack. Twice he was held up by the undead, both times incapacitating them with the greatest economy of effort he could manage. Towards the rear of the vessel there were fewer combatants, as if some force were repelling humans and zombies alike from this region. He seemed to be leaving the mêleé of the battle behind him, although all around he could see Durenese vessels locked in combat with the fleet of the walking dead.

He stepped lightly around the corpse of a young soldier; her long hair, the colour of midnight, was strewn out on the deck behind her shattered face. There was a clear area now between him and the base of the sinister tower. If he could sprint across it as fast as he . . .

"By the belly and lights of the Nameless God!" came a hoarse, rasping whisper, just to his right. "It's my old shipmate, Lone Wolf! How are you, boy?"

He whipped the Sommerswerd round and found himself staring at an empty doorway. Standing in it, crooked, twisting and swaying, was one of the undead, its uniform in tatters, its chest covered with peeling gilt braid.

"Kelman!"

"None other." The voice was a parody of the booming tones Lone Wolf had known while the man was still alive. "It takes more than the waters of the Gulf of Durenor to slay an old sea-hound like me. And call me 'Captain' Kelman, if you please. We may not take much into the next life, but at least we can cling to the ranks we've been given in this one."

"What's happened to you?" Some sea creature had eaten away Kelman's lips. Even as Lone Wolf watched, a few more bristly hairs from the once-luxuriant beard fell from the clammy grip of the man's flaccid flesh.

"Aye, and if Naar's very own giblets were looking at me now, but isn't it obvious? I paid my debts to you, Lone Wolf, like the honest man I am—was—and then I let myself go to the bottom of the sea. And there I was feasted upon by the fishes until I was called back to this ship. Far grander than the *Green Sceptre*, it is, though I

152

confess that I preferred my old vessel; she was little to look at, but I loved every last nail in her timbers."

"Why are you here?"

"To speak with you, my boy. Just to speak with you."

"Why?"

"Put down that sword and I'll tell you. You've got nothing to fear from an old friend like me."

Reluctantly, Lone Wolf lowered the Sommerswerd, so that its point rested on the deck, but he didn't let go of the hilt. He remembered the hopeless manner of Kelman's dying, and the way that the man had forced himself to keep hold of life long enough to give the bottle containing the Gift of Tongues—to pay his gambling dues—but still . . . that had been the living Kelman. Who knew to what dark master this creature might have sworn its allegiance?

"I find it difficult to trust you, my friend," said Lone Wolf simply.

The captain shrieked and his face contorted. Lone Wolf could see the cords moving under the zombie's grey flesh as Kelman fought his expression back under control.

"By the lungs which once were mine, boy," said Kelman, "I cannot explain to you the agony of the walking dead. Every step we take is like blunt knives delving deeply into our stomachs, and every false breath is a fire behind our eyes. Pain is more than just something we feel; it's the whole world to us. The tiniest fragment of a second is an eternity of torment for us."

Lone Wolf glanced over his shoulder, in case more of the zombies might be creeping up behind him, but the deck was empty.

"I can't help you," he said miserably.

"Aye, young boy, but you can. Put away that weapon from you, and my soul will be released from this existence. Put it away now, I tell you!"

Something of Kelman's old bombast had returned to his voice, but still Lone Wolf kept hold of the Sommerswerd. His emotions were in chaos. This was the man who had told him about the game of Life, who had saved him when the crew of the *Green Sceptre* would willingly have strung him from the highest yard-arm—and yet he wasn't a man at all: he was a creature conjured up by Vonotar to walk for one last tortured time among the living.

"I can't *trust* you," he repeated. His eyes were watering. "This sword is mine, and I must keep it by me."

"Then, boy, you must die."

The thing which had once been Kelman fumbled inside the jacket of its uniform. When the wrinkled hand re-emerged it was clasping a black Giak dagger.

"I'd hoped this wouldn't happen," croaked the zombie's voice.

"Don't make me do this," said Lone Wolf. He was suddenly quite calm. "I remember you as my . . . ayeh!"

The dagger had struck him in the hip, and the scorching pain shot through him.

He brought the Sommerswerd up from the deck and struck Kelman—*no, no,* he thought, *not Kelman but the empty frame that used to house Kelman's soul*—beneath the jaw. The swiftly moving blade scooped out the dead captain's tongue. He pulled the sword away and jabbed blindly at his undead friend, his eyes now so filled with tears that he could see nothing more than a blur. Again and again he struck. He felt the sword plunging through dead flesh, but he had little idea of what he was doing.

When his vision finally cleared he found himself standing in the centre of a circle of . . . bits. There was nothing left that was recognizable as having once been a part of his friend, just decaying pieces slowly evaporating in the cold sunlight.

He looked up, remembering a man who had once been his friend, and saw that he was being watched by something that had once—long ago—been Brel.

"Do I have to do this to you, too?" Lone Wolf whispered, miserably.

154

"There should have been no need to be doing that," the undead seaman responded. It seemed to be struggling inwardly.

Lone Wolf misunderstood at first, but then realized that the zombie was telling him that it was trying not to attack him. The memory of its one-time friendship with Lone Wolf must be trying to overrule the magical command to destroy the Durenese and, above all, the last of the Kai. And curiously Lone Wolf found that he trusted Brel's instincts where he had been unable to trust Kelman's.

"I'm sorry," he found himself saying.

"War should have been a bad business," Brel agreed. "I shouldn't be blaming you. But Kelman should have been a good man when he still should have been living." The zombie gestured expressively at the fragments of diseased flesh lying all around them. Its hands clenched and unclenched, as if it were forcing itself not to leap forwards and clamp them murderously around Lone Wolf's neck. "I should have been grieving for him."

"I grieve for him, too," said Lone Wolf. "He was a fine person, in the days when he was still alive."

Lone Wolf had no idea how long the undead seaman would be able to control the demands of whatever evil entity was animating its actions. He left Brel sorrowing over the remains of his captain and moved rapidly across the clear area of deck, shaking his head as if to shake away the memory of Kelman. Echoing in his mind was the sound of the captain yelling ferociously at his crew, barking loudly so that he would never have to bite. Lone Wolf pushed back the bitterness that threatened to engulf him. He reminded himself that he hadn't killed the man, simply released him from the torture of being one of the walking dead, but this was an intellectual reaction, and he recognized it as such; it did little to negate the pain of what he had just done.

Two of the undead came into view, trying to block his path. He hardly thought as he sundered them with the

155

Sommerswerd. He crouched in the door of the tower, gazing upwards through the meshes of a spiral staircase. The metal meshes of the steps obscured his view, but he could just make out a robe of crimson. Then he saw also a twisted back and a shock of straggling white hair.

Vonotar!

Lone Wolf knew who it was without having to think. He had seen the sorcerer the night before, as his own soul and the Sommerswerd's had stabbed into the heart of the world, and he recognized the crooked and ancient man at once.

He crept up the metal stairs, the Sommerswerd before him.

Silently he moved into the uppermost room of the tower. Vonotar had heard nothing. The wizened magician was clutching a black staff, directing it here and there, giggling as washes of flame leaped out from its tip to swamp the Durenese vessels.

Behind him was a Giak. He looked at Lone Wolf hungrily.

"Master . . . " said the Giak, " . . . someone . . . comes . . . among us."

"Shut up, Carag!" Vonotar shouted.

"I . . . think . . . not . . . friend."

"Quiet, beast!"

The magician was wearing a tall curved hat which bore the emblem of a coiled serpent. Lone Wolf remembered the tattoos he had seen on the wrists of the assassins in the Good Cheer Inn and of the false priest, Parsion. He cursed under his breath: the vision he had shared with the Sommerswerd had not told him a lie: this was the foe who had been dogging his footsteps ever since he had left for Hammerdal.

Banedon, he suddenly recalled, Banedon too had been a member of the Brotherhood of the Crystal Star. Could it be possible that Banedon had been acting in concert with Vonotar? No, he couldn't believe it: apart from anything else, he didn't think that the callow boy would

156

have the guts to ally himself with Zagarna. This was the real enemy in front of him—Lone Wolf knew it. The twisted back was towards him . . . it would take only one thrust of the Sommerswerd to end the sorcerer's life forever . . .

"Suggest . . . strongly . . . you . . . turn . . . around, master. This . . . man . . . not . . . friend of ours."

"Carag, I'll—*you!*"

There was so much venom in the last word that Lone Wolf reeled.

He recovered himself swiftly.

"Yes, it's me, Vonotar," he said. "I know you for what you are."

"Know me?" the magician cried. He threw away the black staff he had been holding and stared at Lone Wolf with unabated hatred. The flames of his eyes shone a penetrating blue. "But you've never seen me before."

"I have. We talked last night. Don't you remember?"

Vonotar recalled his disturbed sleep. On his rough bunk in Kaag he had felt as if part of himself had been stolen away. This puppy—this boy who should have died days ago—had invaded him! He spat on the sodden planks of the floor.

"I . . . kill . . . now . . . master?"

"No," said Vonotar. "This is one pleasure I wish to reserve for myself."

The sorcerer sprang to a far corner of the room, raising his hands up in front of his face. He moulded his thoughts to create a Nadziranim spell, and it sparked towards Lone Wolf, burning up the air between them.

"I shall delight in your death, boy," said Vonotar, his voice echoing that of the undead Kelman.

The flash of orange flame halted in the air between them. Lone Wolf felt a judder in the Sommerswerd, and realized that it was repelling the spell which Vonotar had hurled towards them.

"So it was you who spoke through Kelman!"

"But of course. Could I do anything else?"

Lone Wolf felt a vulpine howl of fury bubbling towards his lips. This was the man who had taken over the corpse of his friend; this was the foul fiend who had betrayed Sommerlund to the forces of Darkness.

"I spit upon your soul," he snarled, now more animal than human.

The orange flame moved again, but now it twisted in mid-air and buried itself in the blade of the Sommerswerd. Lone Wolf felt nothing: the weapon had absorbed the darkness of Vonotar's magic, nullifying it with its soul-stuff, burying it away in some unfathomable plane of existence.

"You defy me?" Vonotar's eyes flickered whitely.

"I defy you, and I defy all of your vileness."

"Other days will come."

"What other days?"

"Days when your"—a disdainful wave at the Sommerswerd—"your *artefact* will be unable to protect you from my power."

"I don't think those days will ever be," said Lone Wolf. He was aware that his voice was now low and guttural, and that his lips had drawn back to expose his teeth; the bloodlust he had felt so often in battle was upon him now, and he relished its presence.

Vonotar directed another lance of Nadziranim light towards him, and once again it was swallowed by the Sommerswerd. The little Giak was cowering in one corner, his mind in a tangle: Vonotar had told him that he was invincible, and yet here was someone facing down his master; the situation was too complicated for Carag's simple brain to comprehend.

"Boy!" the sorcerer spat, his eyes blazing, the single word a curse drawn from Naar's own soul. "Soon I will watch with the greatest of pleasure as you breathe your last!"

"But not today. Today you've discovered that your magic is not all-powerful. Today you'll retreat, taking

158

your infernal fleet with you."

"Today is only twenty-four hours. Tomorrow there'll be another day. And then another and another. On one of them you'll meet your doom, you petty . . . "

Vonotar reached up into his headdress and plucked from it a green jewel. Before Lone Wolf could move the sorcerer had thrown the gem down on the caulked deck between them.

The room lit up, and then was filled with choking green gas. Lone Wolf shattered a window to his right with the Sommerswerd, desperate to allow the clean air in, but the freshness didn't come quickly enough. Coughing and spluttering, his vision in a whirl, he stumbled down the spiral staircase, trying to wave away the poisonous vapours from his face.

And then he was out on the clear deck, his sight clearing. His whole mind was blurred with his hatred for Vonotar, and in a frenzy he assaulted the empty air with the Sommerswerd, screaming curses.

"Vengeance!" he shouted at the silent sky. "Vengeance —I swear it will be mine, Vonotar!"

He saw the sorcerer paddling a small boat away from the flagship, the little Giak helping enthusiastically. Then he saw him encircled by a globe of freezing light, moving with preternatural swiftness among the clouds. Next he saw Vonotar atop the highest mast of the Durenese fleet. Wherever he looked, he saw the wizard's mocking skull of a face jeering at him. Now he was leaping nimbly across the corpses floating in the water, using them as stepping stones. Next he was a tracery of clouds in the high heavens, his crimson-coloured robe forming the arch of the sky. A fluttering standard caught Lone Wolf's eye, and he saw that this, too, was Vonotar.

"Number your days, wizard!"

The seas reached themselves up towards the skies, and all came together to form a mouth that laughed mockingly at Lone Wolf.

"You are doomed, child . . . doomed."

8

Somehow Lone Wolf left the flagship of the dead fleet; he was never afterwards able to recall exactly how he did so, although he had a vague memory of slaughtering a pair of Drakkarim with such ease that they might as well have been tiny mosquitoes. The next that he really knew he was jumping to the deck of one of the Durenese warships, the *Kalkarm*, and staggering into the arms of a robust sailor.

Lone Wolf was gibbering meaninglessly, but the sailor soothed him.

Clearly there had been much bloodshed here, but the crew and the soldiers had successfully fought back the undead, and were now cutting loose the grappling ropes which the occupants of the rotting hulk had cast on board. Lone Wolf pulled away from the sailor and leaned against the guard-rail, retching uncontrollably into the dark waters beneath.

Footsteps approached him and he looked up numbly.

Standing there was Axim, his face covered with blood and his armour and shield dented and battered.

"We've won, Lone Wolf," the warrior said. There was deep sorrow in his voice.

"Won? And for what?"

"We've won for Sommerlund, of course," the man said mildly. "Many of us have died today to save this world from conquest by Evil. The enemy is being routed."

Lone Wolf looked out to sea. The vast hulk of the dead fleet's flagship was slowly sinking under a pyre of flames that reached hundreds of feet into the sky. As the vessel slowly went down so, too, did the others of its armada. In his mind he could hear the susurrating moaning of the undead crews as, once again, they returned to the depths from which Vonotar's magic had dragged them.

"But I failed to slay Vonotar," he muttered.

"Vonotar? Who is that?"

Lone Wolf explained, his words stuttering and chopped at first, but then becoming a more fluent stream. He told how he had encountered, on the death-hulk, the same wizard who had been in his vision of the night before.

"He'll return to plague us," said Axim at length.

"That he will. He must have joined forces with Zagarna and taken up the way of right-handed magic. It's a sad day for the Brotherhood of the Crystal Star."

"It's a sadder day for us, Lone Wolf."

"What do you mean?"

"Your friend . . . our friend . . . *my* friend: she's dead."

"Viveka?"

"The same."

There was a silence between them before Lone Wolf spoke again.

"What happened?" he said dully.

"I never trusted her," the warrior said heavily, moving to lean on the rail beside Lone Wolf. "You must have known that. I'm not such a fine actor that I could have concealed it. And yet—and yet my suspicions were ill placed."

He breathed a deep sigh.

"I was fighting a Drakkarim, on this very deck, and the thing was having the better of it. No, that's far too gentle a way of saying it. The creature had me by the neck, and it was drawing its dagger back for the kill when Viveka came out of nowhere and attacked it."

Axim looked out to sea, to where the last of the hulks was slowly sinking beneath the waves.

"She never had a chance, of course. I was groggy from my wounds, and it took me a while to find my feet. When I could see, the life was being sucked out of her throat by that . . . "

He beat his clenched fist cruelly on the rail.

"I killed it. Aye, I ran up behind it and I split its head

161

asunder with my sword, and in the course of time it finally died, but by then she was overboard."

Lone Wolf could see that there were tears in Axim's eyes. He looked self-consciously away, at the waves, at the bloodstained deck—anywhere except at the warrior's face.

"You loved her, Axim. Didn't you?" His voice was hardly more than a whisper. "For all the way that the two of you spat at each other, there was love between you, wasn't there?"

The elderly soldier swallowed.

When he spoke, his voice was barely under control.

"I hadn't seen her for some years when she came to Hammerdal," he said. "She'd taken a fee to kill my nephew and I hated her for it. I'd thrown her out of my life, as if she were a rag that had wrapped itself around my ankles one day as I was walking along the street—thrown her into the gutter, to let her live or die as the Gods decided. I thought I'd forgotten her, but then when I saw her face again I realized that I hadn't."

Lone Wolf couldn't find any words, of grief or reassurance or sympathy. He remembered how vibrant and living Viveka had been, the firmness of her as she had lain nestled close to him on the couch at King Alin's court, her wisdom in turning him back from her room. He yearned to hear her voice again, to know that she was somewhere nearby. But he knew that he never would. Her body must be lost to the waves by now, her fine hair tangled and wet in the cold waters.

"She was your lover?" he said.

"No."

Axim turned to look at him. The soldier was not ashamed of the tears flowing easily now from his eyes.

"No. I thought you'd guessed, Lone Wolf. Viveka wasn't my lover. She was my daughter."

6

THE RETURN OF THE KAI

1

The tales are told and the songs are sung of the time that Lone Wolf led the Durenese fleet to Holmgard, and of the part that the Lady Qinefer played on that day. Blood was shed and great was the valour of the Sommlending and the Durenese. We who follow after can only marvel at the courage of our ancestors, and pray to Ishir and Kai that, should ever we be called upon to face Evil, we, too, will acquit ourselves as well . . .

2

Of the seventy Durenese warships that had left Port Bax, only about fifty had survived the battle of the fleet of the dead. It was impossible to estimate how many men and women had lost their lives—perhaps as many as five thousand. Among the dead was Calfen: the little admiral had been spitted by an arrow moments after the two fleets had joined battle. Lone Wolf went through the formalities of mourning the man's loss, but his heart wasn't in it: he was numbed by the fact that Viveka was dead. As he walked the decks of the *Kalkarm*, supervising the work of repair, he found himself constantly looking up, expecting to see her clear eyes on him, or to hear her curiously girlish laugh. It was as if some fundamental part of him refused point-blank to believe that she was dead.

In the absence of Calfen, Axim had taken control of the fleet, with the *Kalkarm* as his flagship. For the next thirty-six hours, Lone Wolf saw very little of his Durenese friend, who was busy organizing the repair of the fleet while at the same time making sure that they kept up full speed for Holmgard. Lone Wolf spent the time wandering the decks, speaking with the crewmen as they worked, chatting with the soldiers and trying to make himself feel as if he were doing something useful. He was delighted to find that morale among the remaining warriors was high, despite the heavy losses the army had sustained. The men and women were in a mood of great confidence. They had battled with the forces of the living dead, had they not? Surely it would then be no more than child's play to rout Zagarna's hosts? Lone Wolf carefully forbore from telling them that Giaks, Gourgaz, Kraan, Doomwolves, Helghast, Zlanbeast and Xaghash were no mean foes: better that the troops faced the coming battle in a mood of bright optimism than that they confronted the Darklord's army filled with the conviction that they were just so much battle-fodder. Besides, there was a mist in his mind, shielding him from a true remembrance of what Zagarna's hordes were really like.

He had got into the habit of speaking to the Sommerswerd. He tried to conceal this from the other people aboard the *Kalkarm*, but he suspected from the way they looked at him sometimes that he had been observed, and not just once or twice. Yet he couldn't stop himself. The sword was more closely related to him than a blood-brother could have been, and he felt that it answered all the questions that he asked of it. He couldn't put its answers into words, but they seemed complete enough to him.

He was aware, also, that time didn't seem to be following its usual course. The only way that he could tell whether it was morning or evening was to look at the sky, and even then his guess was often wrong. He was never hungry; when it seemed to him that too long a time had passed since last he'd had a meal, he forced himself to eat, but he gained no satisfaction from the food, and he was able to finish only a little bit of it. He slept whenever and wherever the mood took him, curling up, more often than not, on a coil of rope on the deck rather than in the cabin which had been allotted to him. Occasionally he wondered if he should wash, but the moment never seemed right and so he didn't bother. He was vaguely conscious of the fact that his mind wasn't functioning properly but this—like so many other things—was a matter which he decided just to push away from him, to think about another day.

The only thing which he conscientiously remembered to do was to keep up to date his record of the number of days he had been away from Holmgard. He couldn't rightly remember exactly why this was important, but he was certain that it was. On a sheet of parchment which he had brought from Hammerdal he scored a line for each day that passed. There was the evening of the battle against the dead: that was easy enough to remember. Then there was another day, and as darkness fell he couldn't remember whether it had been the same day as the battle or a different one; but he made a mark to record its passage anyway. Things became a bit of a jumble after that, but he felt certain, as he stood late one afternoon watching the spires of Holmgard come into view on the distant horizon, that this was the thirty-seventh day since he had left the city. He had a murky recollection that he had been told to return within forty days, but for the life of him he couldn't remember why.

The spell was broken as he stood on the *Kalkarm*'s

deck watching distant Holmgard.

"Lone Wolf!" A clap across his shoulders. Axim was beside him, sharing his view out across the water.

Memories rushed back into his mind, and he staggered. It was as if he had been wrapped in a blanket the past couple of days and now someone had dragged it away from his face so that the sunlight was stabbing into his eyes.

"We'll get there under cover of night," the warrior remarked, oblivious to Lone Wolf's mental turmoil. "There's no moon tonight, so we should be able to slip in undetected by Zagarna's horde."

"Yes—yes—that sounds fine." His thoughts were like a whirlpool. All of his memories were clear enough in themselves, but they were refusing to settle down into the right order.

"We'll scatter them easily," Axim was saying. "Our troops are eager for the fray. Those spawn won't know what's hit them."

His nose jutted out proudly, matching the prow of the ship, and Lone Wolf hid a smile.

"I hope you're right," he said, pulling his mind forcibly back into focus. *What have I been doing these past days? Was it that Vonotar was snaring me in yet another of his evil ensorcellments? Or was it just that . . . she's dead. Viveka's dead. I'll never see her again. Whatever she was in the life she had when I didn't know her, she was a fine person. She had a wisdom that I don't yet have. She . . . oh, Viveka, Viveka, why did you have to damn well die?*

"Don't worry," said Axim. "Of course I'm right. Wait 'til those Giaks get a taste of hard Durenese steel—they'll turn their tails and flee from us, I can promise you."

"Giaks are tough," said Lone Wolf, patting the older man on the forearm, "and Kraan are even tougher. Don't speak too soon, my friend." *I can still feel her lips touching mine, and the way that she pushed me away so gently.*

"You know something?" said Axim gravely, turning to look at him. "You worry too much, far too much, Lone Wolf."

166

In a way Lone Wolf agreed with the warrior; at the same time he recognized the danger of the man's seeming euphoria. The army they bore with them was a fine one—no doubt of that—but it might easily find its match when ranged against the spawn under Zagarna's command. And, of course, Vonotar might be there, too, and who could tell what the sorcerer might try to do?

Lone Wolf tried to convey something of these thoughts to Axim, but the warrior refused to listen, consciously shrugging away the words.

"I have to leave you now," he said after a while. "I never realized how demanding the job of being an admiral is. I wish that Calfen were still with us."

And I wish that your daughter were still with us, thought Lone Wolf sadly, *but I don't suppose I could ever tell you how much I wished that.*

3

Qinefer was standing high on one of the many towers of Holmgard's outer earthworks, gazing towards the sea. Now that it was night, the clash of battle had abated. Behind her she could hear the mutterings and gruntings of King Ulnar's troops as they settled down; ahead of her there was a very similar mumbling as Zagarna's spawn, too, gave it up for the night. She was reminded for the thousandth time of the fact that the Darklord's spawn were in many ways so much like humans—caricatures of humans, perhaps. Her brown eyes swept across the blankness of the dark ocean. A ball of flaming rags, catapulted from beyond the city walls, had just passed her view, and it took a few moments for her vision to accommodate once more to the darkness.

There was a light out there. She was certain of it. Her first reaction was that Zagarna must at last be bringing a navy to torment the battered city, but then she thought again: if the Darklord had had a fleet, surely he would have deployed it by now. The light vanished, and there was nothing but blackness out there. Perhaps a sailor had been lighting his pipe?

It had been more than a month since Lone Wolf had left, and most nights she had wished that she were travelling in his place. She had never seen him in combat, but she had supreme confidence in her own abilities: was she not the woman who had slain two Gourgaz in a single day? She doubted that Lone Wolf could have done as much.

There was another gleam from the purple blackness of the gulf. *The fools!* she thought. *It only takes one Giak to look out that way and . . .*

A furore erupted below her. She looked down, clipping her sword anxiously against her thigh, irritated by the fact that she was expected to wear a cloak of chain. She itched to be dressed once more in the homespun clothes she'd been wearing when first she came to this city.

There was a whisper in the air.

The Durenese are coming. The Durenese are coming. The Durenese are . . .

She refused to let herself become part of the chant, but at the same time she recognized its power. Only— only she knew that the hope of salvation was bleeding her troops: the more that they relied upon this force from beyond the seas, the more that they would expect it to be easy to drive back the siege.

Qinefer put on her helmet decisively. It had become a matter of course that the two armies didn't attack each other at night—except for the fireballs which the besiegers catapulted incessantly into the city—but this was no normal night. She buckled the strap under her chin, and felt the bloodlust beginning to creep into her. She pulled her great broadsword from its sheath and felt it move easily through the calm breeze that came from the Holmgulf.

She clattered down the stone steps that separated the ramparts from the base of the city and began to call up

168

her troops. Most of the men and women came reluctantly, although there were a few whose predatory eagerness frightened even Qinefer. She rallied them around her and briefly explained what she intended to do. While the besieging horde basked secure in the knowledge that the Sommlending would never attack them at night, she wanted to lead a foray out into their camp, slaying as many of the somnolent Giaks and Kraan as possible and shattering any morale they might have for the morrow—the morning when the Durenese would descend upon them, screaming their battle-cries.

It was easy—far too easy, she thought.

Within minutes she was surrounded by a group of enthusiastic volunteers. Most of them were young—some of them even younger than she was—and she felt guilty: they'd be lucky if half of them returned.

She sent a servant to bring Janos from the stables, and pulled herself up on the stallion's broad back. Other horses were led out, and soon her soldiers were mounted behind her. She let out a bloodcurdling yell, and the guards at the city gate threw open the ponderous doors, watching in amazement as Qinefer's small army pounded by them.

The next two hours were unrelieved misery. Qinefer lost count of the number of times that her sword had descended to sunder half-awake Giaks; she inured herself to their dying screams. The Kraan were even easier prey: the great bat-like creatures were somnolent and hardly able to pull themselves up into the air; hundreds of them died on the swords of Qinefer's troops, their greenish innards spattering slickly across the mud. The sight sickened Qinefer, but she knew that she couldn't let the fact show: her troops would lose all their confidence in her if they suspected her of weakness.

The raid lasted only about a quarter of an hour, but it served its purpose. Qinefer and her soldiers galloped back through the gates of Holmgard, hearing the heavy wooden panels closing behind them. She raised her vizor and grinned at the men and women milling on their horses around her.

"Victory?" she said, very quietly, but the word was passed from one person to the next.

"Victory!" came a great chorus of voices. "Victory!"

Ah, yes, thought Qinefer, *but what'll it be like tomorrow?*

4

The Durenese ships slipped easily into the port of Holmgard. A few drunken men, staggering hopelessly along the quay, saw the ships arrive, but otherwise they went largely unobserved. Later a sailor would tell his wife that he had seen a fleet of ghosts arrive in the port, but she would shush him to sleep, telling him that the wanlo which he shouldn't have been drinking had created phantasms in his mind.

The sailor pushed himself further down into his bed and assumed that his wife was correct. He had only the dimmest memories of the evening. It was quite likely that he'd been mistaken when he'd thought he'd seen fifty or more warships moving smoothly into the harbour. It was . . . but then he was embraced in sleep's warm arms.

The few sober men and women who had seen the arrival of the Durenese fleet at first assumed that it had been sent by the Darklord Zagarna; they fled yelling through the streets, rousing their neighbours. A throng of Holmgard citizens, murmuring angrily, gathered on the dockside, bearing sharp kitchen-knives and gardening implements. Minutes later, a detachment of cavalry arrived from King Ulnar's palace to calm the situation, and soon the vengeful mutterings had turned into rousing cheers.

The boarding-ramps of the *Kalkarm* were hoisted down to rest on the harbour-side. First to come down it was an honour guard of Durenese soldiers, and then Axim gravely led Lone Wolf down the narrow board. The cheering of the assembled citizens became overpowering, and now they took up a new chant: "The Kai Lord has returned—the return of the Kai!" Lone Wolf held the Sommerswerd high above his head, and it throbbed with its own golden light.

The leader of the cavalry approached, holding a blazing torch above her head and leading an extra horse alongside her own. He recognized it immediately as Janos, his old friend, the gift of Prince Pelathar. Instinct made Lone Wolf look at the rider's face; Qinefer put out her tongue at him as he sheathed the Sommerswerd and climbed into the saddle. Her tired face wrinkled in a friendly smile, as she whispered, just loud enough so that he could hear her above the roar of the crowd: "Well done, Kai. Almost as well as I could have done it myself."

He knew the gravity of the situation, but he couldn't stop himself from chuckling.

"Well, next time *you* do it, then."

"Is that a promise?"

Lone Wolf didn't answer. He could feel the Sommerswerd pulling urgently at his hip. It was trying to draw him away from the harbour, towards the centre of Holmgard.

He gestured, and Qinefer immediately understood. She issued a few sharp orders to the cavalry under her command, and they swiftly cleared a way through the teeming mob.

Lone Wolf saluted Axim sombrely, and the warrior stood erect, his head proud, and equally gravely returned the salute. Then Qinefer and Lone Wolf turned their horses and rode off through the wall of noise.

Soon they had left the crowds behind and were clattering rapidly through the deserted streets of the city, guided by the urgings of the Sommerswerd. Lone Wolf was horrified by the devastation he saw all around them. In the intermittent light of Qinefer's torch it seemed to

171

him that hardly a single building had been left undamaged, and many of them had been reduced to little more than heaps of stones and ash. From time to time they saw corpses lying on the streets, waiting for the night-patrol to clear them away.

She told him of what it had been like in his absence, of how the citizens had had to become used to a diet of fish, rats and domestic pets, of how they had become accustomed to drinking mead, ale and wine because all the remaining water was brackish and foul, of the diseases which had added their own devastation to the assaults of the enemy, of a thousand other miseries of a city under siege. She found time to mention—just as an aside—how she had been able to slaughter not one but two Gourgaz in a single day.

They came to the city's main gate, surmounted by its great dark watchtower. The wood of the gate was charred around the edges, and in places its even surface had been patched with timbers purloined from elsewhere, but the defence had held.

Prompted by the Sommerswerd, Lone Wolf reined in Janos and dismounted.

"From here on I must go alone," he said.

Qinefer felt slighted. However, she nodded resignedly. "Good luck."

"I thank you."

He took a torch from one of the sentries and then turned and ran into the doorway at the base of the watchtower. The Sommerswerd was urging him faster and faster up the spiral stairs. At the very top of the tower there was a small round deck. A couple of watchmen turned as Lone Wolf arrived gasping. They instantly recognized him from his clothing as the returned Kai Lord; they bowed reverently towards him and then left him, their footsteps rattling away down the spiral stairs.

The Sommerswerd was telling Lone Wolf that he was just in time, that dawn was almost breaking. Under its instructions, he knelt down beside the tower's wooden parapet and faced towards the east. He felt the soul-stuff spread out rapidly to become a part of the sword. More than ever before, the two of them became a single entity, a creature acting with one mind, no barriers at all between them any more.

The sky was a wash of pink, yellow and green. Heavy clouds hung over the Holmgulf, and the air was tingling with the threat of a thunderstorm, but at the horizon the sky was clear. Lone Wolf looked out over the vast encampment of Zagarna's army and saw the great red war-tent which the Darklord had had erected for himself; sewn into the crimson fabric was the symbol of a broken skull.

Lone Wolf's lips peeled back. He and the sword together were no longer truly human; mixed within them there was something of the nameless ones but also something of the wolf which had given him his name. They were the solitary member of the pack, the one which hunted on its own. Now was the time to make the kill. His tongue lolled out of his mouth, twitching eagerly from side to side. His body was tensed, crouching, ready to spring.

He took the Sommerswerd and held it out in front of him, the line of its blade pointing directly towards Zagarna's tent. He and the sword waited patiently a few more moments.

And then the first fire of the sun rose above the far horizon. A single shaft of dawn light came across the sea.

Lone Wolf stood, the Sommerswerd still stretched out towards the huge red tent.

The shaft of light touched the very tip of the sword.

Both Lone Wolf and the Sommerswerd became a statue carved out of incandescent white light. The whole of the plain beneath them—and the mud and the tents and the war engines and the embers of the campfires—was suddenly lit more brightly than any day. Some Giaks on their early-morning rounds looked up in awe, their eyes nictitating in the glare.

A thrust of lightning sprang from the Sommerswerd to the Darklord's tent. Thunder shattered the air. The tent vanished, and in its place there was a great column of fire, expanding heavenwards.

All of the world seemed to howl with the anguish of Zagarna's destruction. The heavy clouds over the Holmgulf clashed together. The seas rose and rushed towards the shore. A million voices seemed to be screaming in unison as the mud and rocks of the plain buckled, throwing the spawn from the Darklands high into the air or swallowing them up in greedy fissures. An unearthly golden light flooded the world as far as the eye could see.

And then there was rain—warm, gentle rain.

Lone Wolf sheathed the Sommerswerd, its light now only a subdued red glow, and cupped his hands to the rain.

He tasted the water once, and then again.

And then he fell.

5

It was some days later that messengers brought the news to Toran. They told of how Lone Wolf and the Sommerswerd had destroyed the Darklord, and of how the armies of the Sommlending and the Durenese had driven back the shocked hordes of Zagarna, forcing them into the sea or slaughtering them on the land. They praised the heroism of the Lady Qinefer, and told of how she had led the first storm attack on the spawn, during the night; but most of all they talked of the wonder of the returning Kai, and of his courage and prowess in retrieving the Sommerswerd from Durenor and wielding it to erase Zagarna from the Lastlands.

No one would ever know how many men and women died that day, but for each of them a dozen of the spawn had returned to Naar. Some had escaped into the

174

countryside, only to be hunted down by Sommlending villagers. A few had been carried away by Kraan and Zlanbeast, presumably back to Kaag, but the army from the Darklands had been so heavily defeated that there should never again be any threat from there—at least for a long while, perhaps a lifetime.

The Guildmaster brought the news to Banedon, still engaged in his lonely vigil at Alyss's bedside. The Guildmaster's two kittens fought amicably around their ankles as they talked, and Banedon impulsively threw himself into his mentor's arms, sobbing in happiness that Sommerlund had been saved. Even the Guildmaster found that there were unaccustomed tears in his old grey eyes.

But then Banedon's shoulders ceased heaving and he stood back from the Guildmaster.

"It's not over yet," he said, his voice ragged.

The two of them looked slowly at the narrow cot where Alyss's body lay, swathed in sunlight, motionless, neither dead nor alive.

"No," said the Guildmaster, ignoring the tiny snarls of the kittens at their feet. Somewhere, out there in Aon, Alyss's spirit was still blinded and lost.

"No, it's not over yet."

GLOSSARY

Agarash the Damned Servant of Naar, creator of the Doomstones, slayer of Nyxator. His empire ruled all of Magnamund until he was defeated by the Elder Magi.

Agarashi The "Creatures of Darkness" created by Agarash the Damned. The monstrous semi-sentient and non-sentient monsters which inhabit Magnamund are descendants of Agarash's early creations.

Alin IV, King Ruler of Durenor.

Anskavern Port and province of Sommerlund.

Aon "The Great Balance." Name given to the universe in which Magnamund exists.

Border Rangers Mounted rangers who patrol the borders of Sommerlund.

Brotherhood of the Crystal Star The magicians' Guild of Sommerlund, based in Toran.

Burrowcrawler A subterranean Agarashi found in the Lastlands.

Cloeasia A country bordering Durenor and Vassagonia.

Crypt Spawn Winged creatures which can be summoned at will by all Darklords. They inhabit the Plane of Darkness and can be used to overwhelm an enemy or despoil crops and livestock.

Darklands   The domain of the Darklords. A once-fertile region of Northern Magnamund which the Darklords have transformed into a vast area of harsh, volcanic wasteland.

Darklords   Twenty powerful beings sent by Naar to destroy the Sommlending and conquer Magnamund.

Dazhiarn or **Daziarn**   An astral world which exists outside Aon. Access to the Dazhiarn can be achieved by travel through a Shadow Gate.

Dessi   A tropical realm of Magnamund ruled by the few remaining descendants of the Elder Magi, the race of beings from whom all "left-handed" magic descends.

Doomstones   Powerful artefacts which contain elements of pure Evil. Fashioned by Agarash the Damned in mockery of the Lorestones.

Doomwolves   Ferocious wolf-like spawn created by the Darklords for use as battle mounts for their Giaks.

Drakkarim   Barbaric humanoid race allied to the Darklords.

Durenor   A country to the north-east of Magnamund. Sworn enemy of the Darklords and a loyal ally of the Sommlending.

Durncrag Mountains   Granite mountains which form a natural barrier between Sommerlund and the Darklands.

Elder Magi   Agents of Kai and Ishir who slayed Agarash the Damned. Their numbers were decimated during the Great Plague and now the survivors live in Dessi.

Fehmarn   The first day of Spring. Revered as a holy day by the Sommlending who, upon this day, reaffirm their oath of allegiance to their king.

Fryearl   A highly respected Sommlending title, bestowed by the King on those who have displayed exceptional courage. Elevates the recipient to a rank and title equivalent to those of a Baron.

Fryeman   A Sommlending who has earned the right to relinquish his fealty to a Baron.

Gallowbrush   Deep red thorny briar, commonly called "Sleeptooth." Scratches from its thorns can cause drowsiness.

Giaks   A prolific race of creatures once used as slaves in the construction of Darkland fortresses. Now they form the mainstay of all Darklord armies.

Gourgaz   A race of sentient reptilians who inhabit the Maakenmire Swamp of Northern Magnamund. Carnivorous, with a preference for human flesh. Used by the Darklords to lead Giak battle units.

178

Graveweed A thorny briar from which can be distilled a powerful poison.

Hammerdal The capital city of Durenor.

Helgedad The principal city-fortress of the Darklords.

Helghast Powerful undead beings, originally created by Darklord Vashna in the war against the Sommlending. They can adopt the semblance of human form.

Holmgard The capital city of Sommerlund.

Ishir The Goddess of Good, High Priestess of the Moon. Through her pledge with Naar she brought about the creation of Aon, and by her request she persuaded Kai to send to Magnamund his forces of Good.

Kaag A Darkland city-fortress located 300 miles due west of Holmgard.

Kai The God of Good, Lord of the Sun. Has allied himself with Ishir in an attempt to repel the forces of Evil from Magnamund.

Kai, Order of the The warrior elite of Sommerlund. Its members possess martial and mental disciplines bestowed upon them by the God Kai.

Kalte The icy wasteland located in the northern polar regions of Magnamund.

Kian, King The first Sommlending king, who led his people into the realm now known as Sommerlund, and who in so doing pushed the Darklords back behind the Durncrag Mountains.

Kirlundin Isles A string of islands off the coast of Sommerlund which form a baronial province.

Kraan Large, leathery-winged flying creatures. A sub-species of Zlanbeast used by the Darklords as flying mounts for their Giaks and Vordaks.

Lakuri Isles A subtropical group of islands controlled by Captain Khadro's notorious pirate fleet.

Lastlands A collective term used to describe Sommerlund, Durenor, Cloeasia and the Wildlands.

Laumspur A wild herb with a bright scarlet flower. Much prized for its healing properties.

Lorestones Created by Nyxator, these golden gems encapsulate the wisdom given to him by the God Kai. Later they were to enlighten Sun Eagle, the founder of the Order of the Kai, and enable the development of innate Kai skills within every Sommlending Kai Lord.

Maakengorge A great rift to the south of the Durncrag Mountains. It was here that King Ulnar I of Sommerlund slew Darklord Vashna. The spirit of Vashna still haunts the deep reaches of this gorge.

Maakenmire The swamp home of the Gourgaz.

Magnakai, Book of the A great tome of learning in which Sun Eagle recorded in detail the wisdom he had learned from his study of the Lorestones. After his death, this tome became the principal source of inspiration for successive generations of Kai Lords.

Magnamund A planet of Aon which has become the focus of a battle between the forces of Good and Evil.

Moonstone A gem of great magical power, created by the Shianti in the Dazhiarn Plane, and brought with them to Magnamund. It disturbed the fine balance between Good and Evil and heralded the start of a Golden Age, during which human races first appeared on Magnamund.

Naar The King of Darkness. The ultimate force of Evil within and without Aon.

Nadziranim The magicians employed by the Darklords. Adherents and adepts of the destructive and evil right-handed path of magic.

Naogizaga The "no-lands." A vast volcanic desert of dust which forms the greatest single landmass of the Darklands.

Nyxator First servant of the God of Kai. Nyxator adopted the form of a dragon when he entered Magnamund. First recipient of Kai's wisdom, and creator of the Lorestones.

Pelathar, Prince Crown Prince of Sommerlund, King Ulnar V's only son.

Ragadorn Sleazy Wildlands city-port located at the mouth of the River Dorn.

Raumas Ancient Sommlending forest temple destroyed during the Age of the Black Moon.

Ruanon The southernmost province of Sommerlund, renowned for its mineral wealth.

Shadow Gate A rent in the fabric of time and space which separates Aon from the Dazhiarn. Passage between the two worlds can be effected by stepping through a Shadow Gate.

Shianti A race of nomadic lesser gods, devotees of Ishir, who entered Magnamund in the year 1600 MS. They were worshipped as gods by the early human races, and known by several names— Majhan, Suukon, Ancients. Their Moonstone disrupted the balance of Magnamund until they were persuaded by Ishir to return it to the Dazhiarn. The Shianti exiled themselves to the Isle of Lorn, in Southern Magnamund, and have since vowed to take no further part in the affairs of mankind.

Sommerlund Home of the Sommlending, a naturally fertile country bordered by the Darklands to the west and the Wildlands to the east.

Sommerswerd The Sword of the Sun. A weapon bestowed upon the Sommlending people by Kai, Lord of the Sun, to enable them to do battle with the Darklords. The only weapon (other than those created by the Nadziranim) capable of killing a Darklord. Its inherent power will fade if wielded in combat by any save a Kai Lord.

Sommlending A race of pale-skinned, predominantly fair-haired humans who came to Sommerlund from the Northern Void in the year MS 3434.

Storm Hawk Lone Wolf's first tutor, slain by Vonotar while scouting the Durncrag Mountains.

Sun Eagle The name taken by the first Baron of Toran upon his completion of the first quest for the Lorestones of Nyxator, and his subsequent mastery of the Kai Disciplines. Sun Eagle was the first of the Kai Lords. He founded the Order of the Kai and established the Kai Monastery in western Sommerlund.

Szalls A cowardly breed of Giak found in the Wildlands. Fled there from the Durncrag Mountains to avoid persecution by the stronger Mountain Giaks, now used by the Darklords.

Toran A city-port of Sommerlund located on the northern coast. All of the most important Sommlending guilds are based here.

Tyso A wealthy port and province of Sommerlund which falls under the jurisdiction of Baron Tor Medar, Chancellor of the Realm.

Ulnar V, King The current ruler of Sommerlund, direct descendant of Ulnar I, slayer of Vashna.

Vashna The most powerful of the twenty Darklords created by Naar. Masterminded the invasion of Magnamund that was to secure the region now known as the Darklands. During a war with the Sommlending, he was destroyed by King Ulnar I and the Sommerswerd in a duel fought on the brink of the Maakengorge.

Vassagonia A rich desert empire situated in northern Magnamund. Its policy of ruthless imperialism has brought it into conflict with most of its neighbouring states.

Vordak Silicon-based undead creatures, the first to be summoned and controlled by Vashna during his early experiments in the dungeons of Helgedad. Used as lieutenants in the armies of the Darklords.

Wildlands An area of wasteland situated to the south-east of Sommerlund. Formerly part of Cloeasia, this region was laid to waste during the formation of the Maakengorge and the subsequent geological upheaval. Ragadorn, by virtue of its coastal location, was the only city to survive.

Xaghash Powerful lesser Darklords who occupy the courts of Helgedad. To maintain their physical strength they are obliged to devour warm-blooded creatures (preferably humans). Many of the raids launched from the Darklands are for the purpose of gathering "food" for the Xaghash.

Zlanbeast Large flying creatures, used as air transport by the armies of the Darklords. The largest species, the Imperial Zlanbeast, are used as personal mounts by the Darklords of Helgedad.